Her eyes met his, finally.

He ran his fingertips where her dimples showed when she smiled. Bree wasn't smiling now. "Why are you sorry?"

"Because I have feelings for you. Because I'm leaving soon."

Hearing her admit she cared did something to him. Something he didn't expect. Something he didn't want to lose. "Do you really have to go way out to Seattle?"

"Don't even think of asking me to stay."

He didn't want to let this die, but then, what kind of chance did they have? "We can keep in touch."

That sounded lame, even to his ears. They'd known each other a couple of weeks but it was long enough to have feelings for each other. Real feelings he should know better than to pursue. Hadn't he learned that whirlwind romances didn't last?

Glancing at Bree's hand wrapped firmly in his own made him wonder if maybe they could—with the right woman.

Bree was real and she cared. Problem was, he didn't want her to leave. But if he asked her to stay, he might lose her forever.

Jenna Mindel lives in northwest Michigan with her husband and their three dogs. A 2006 Romance Writers of America RITA® Award finalist, Jenna has answered her heart's call to write inspirational romances set near the Great Lakes.

Books by Jenna Mindel

Love Inspired

Maple Springs

Falling for the Mom-to-Be
A Soldier's Valentine
A Temporary Courtship

Big Sky Centennial

His Montana Homecoming

Mending Fences
Season of Dreams
Courting Hope
Season of Redemption
The Deputy's New Family

A Temporary Courtship

Jenna Mindel

HARLEQUIN® LOVE INSPIRED®

Recycling programs
for this product may
not exist in your area.

LOVE INSPIRED BOOKS

ISBN-13: 978-0-373-71985-3

A Temporary Courtship

Copyright © 2016 by Jenna Mindel

www.Harlequin.com

Printed in U.S.A.

Then the LORD God said,
"It is not good that the man should be alone;
I will make him a helper fit for him."
—*Genesis* 2:18

To my husband, for supporting my dream.
I love you!

Chapter One

Conservation officer Darren Zelinsky blew out his breath and stared at the Bay Willows Association community building. He'd been here more times than he cared to remember with Raleigh, the woman he'd once planned to marry. He wasn't here today by choice either.

Bay Willows was a private summer resort located within his hometown of Maple Springs, Michigan. The large white two-story Victorian structure before him, complete with a broad porch on one side, reminded him of what he'd lost. And what he hoped to gain by coming here.

Ice cream socials were held on that porch. The last time he'd been to an ice cream social two years ago with his girl, it had taken every ounce of willpower to play nice with people he'd resented since he was kid. People who'd looked down their noses at a local, making him feel like an awkward teen trying to protect his turf.

Darren had Local Yokel stamped on his forehead, and that wasn't ever going to change. He didn't want it to. He loved not only Maple Springs but also the entire Tip of the Mitt. It was why he was so good at his job with the state's Department of Natural Resources.

The late April afternoon had turned warm and sunny.

A perfect day for mushrooming. Teri, his supervisor, had asked him to fill in for her wild edibles class. This wasn't for fun, it was work. This was the opportunity he needed, too, because he wanted her job.

Rumor had it that Teri might not return from maternity leave with her late-in-life surprise baby. He'd also heard that her husband relocated to the town they'd come from downstate. Good news for Darren. He didn't want to come in second place this time. The supervisor job should have been his over two years ago, but his regional boss had gone with Teri instead, a more seasoned CO several years older than Darren. Teri was used to dealing with a more diverse population.

He glanced around the area he'd avoided for nearly two years. He had to prove himself here. Prove he had what it took to get along with these people. But so many bad memories resided here, alongside these beautiful people.

Most cottages remained shut up for winter. The majority of summer residents arrived in time for Memorial Day, a month away yet. Summertime in Maple Springs was gorgeous, but with the beauty came the crowds. His town swelled with part-timers and tourists overtaking the shops and sidewalks and slowing down traffic.

Bay Willows threw open her gates on April 1. Half a dozen or so of those early residents had signed up for this class. Every week for the next few, Darren would instruct uppity summer residents how not only to prepare but also to find wild edibles. He was more than qualified. He'd been scouring the woods since he was a kid. He knew where to find everything Teri had planned before her doctor called her out.

Farm to table was big right now, and foraging for local fare had become an *in* thing. If there was one thing he'd learned about Bay Willows, being *in* was important. Darren had never been one for fads or passing fancies. Safety was his thing. Protecting the area he loved.

But God had a funny way of making a man face his past. And his failures. So here Darren stood in front of the Bay Willows community building, a place he'd vowed never to step foot in again, hoping to somehow rewind history. He wanted a different outcome this time. He'd not only get the job he wanted but also get over Raleigh, banishing her from his soul so he could move on.

She wouldn't be here. She'd hated these kinds of things, calling the classes and workshops given by Bay Willows "hokey gatherings for bored housewives and grandmothers." She'd had a rebellious streak when it came to this place, disdaining it almost as much as he. Maybe that was what had made him attractive to her in the first place. He didn't belong here and Raleigh knew that, but he hadn't been good enough to keep. In the end, she'd left him.

Music tugged his attention away from his dark thoughts. String music. A violin?

"Good. Now pick up the pace. Like this," a woman's voice, muffled and barely discernible, encouraged.

He heard a deeper string sound emanate from above, streaming out an open second-floor window like a soft spring rain. Mellow and warm, the song wrapped around him. For a moment, he forgot why he didn't want to be here. Even his plan to go over the class notes one more time faded away as he simply listened.

The violin joined in, trying to keep up. Whoever played the deeper sounding instrument was good. Really good. The music suddenly stopped, followed by the scrape of a chair. "Sorry, but I've got to run." A pause and then, "Let me know if you need help."

He couldn't hear the response. Whoever played the violin kept going, but the richer-sounding instrument was done. *Bummer*. It wasn't a bass. What were those things called…

Darren shifted his satchel and focused on the double doors ahead. Time to go to work. He took one more sweeping look around the clump of a few buildings that made up the Bay Willows administrative campus in the midst of summer cottages arranged by the lake. Confident his ex-fiancée wasn't lurking in the shadows, Darren stepped inside.

The community room had a kitchen where he'd demonstrate how to prepare what they found in the field. He took over a table at the front of the main room and pulled out the required paperwork. Liability waivers, emergency contact information and wild edible booklets for each attendee along with a calendar of class topics and a list of suggested items to bring on each outing. He was as ready as he'd ever be.

"Mr. Zelinsky?"

He jerked his head up at the sound of a feminine voice. "Yes?"

A slight woman with dark brown hair framing a pretty face stood before him, scattering his thoughts. She was average height but delicate-looking; her full lips stained red made her creamy skin look that much lighter. Her bangs had been cut short and jagged as if she'd let a kid loose with scissors. His sisters had had dolls with choppy bangs like that by the time they'd gotten done with them. The rest of the woman's thick hair was long and straight.

Her eyes were a wild golden color framed by dark lashes, putting him in mind of the bobcat he'd come upon last winter. No eye makeup, as far as he could tell; she didn't need it. She stepped closer and held out her hand. "Bree Anderson. My mother, Joan, organized this class, but she's off her feet with a broken ankle, so I'm here to help."

Momentarily mesmerized by those eyes, he didn't take her offered hand. "Help?"

She looked at him like he might be dim-witted—the typical local boy without a brain. "You know, help with anything you may need since you're sort of filling in at the last minute."

He'd had a good week's notice. Plenty of time. "What did you say your name was?"

"Bree. Bree Anderson." She let her hand drop.

On the edge of uppity, the name suited her. Bree Anderson looked exactly like what he'd expect. *Pampered*, *sheltered* and *expensive* were written all over her.

"Like the cheese?" He threw out that verbal jab without thinking.

Amusement shone from Bree's eyes instead of offense. Her mouth lifted, making deep dimples in her cheeks. One more thing to tease him. "Yes. Exactly like the cheese but with two *e*'s and no *i*."

She had a slight lilt in her voice. Not a prominent accent or anything, simply a different way of enunciating certain words that made it obvious she wasn't from around here.

"Got it. My name's Darren." He handed over the forms. She'd be his liaison, then, the link between a backward local and the *in* summer folk. "You might as well read and sign these. Everyone needs to complete them before we go anywhere. Let me know if you have any questions."

"Sure thing." She bit the top of the pen as she read over the forms. Straight white teeth were framed by those full, bow-shaped red lips. Who wore red lipstick?

Who cared? He liked it.

Tightening his jaw, he turned away. He needed to stop noticing things about her, now. Noticing led to attraction, and that could only lead to trouble. Darren had had enough trouble with one woman from Bay Willows to last a lifetime.

Bree signed her name in a tight scrawl and handed over the waiver. "Seems self-explanatory. Seek and eat at our own risk."

"Exactly." He took the signed forms without looking at her.

"Darren, is that you?"

His heart pitched when he heard that voice. Of course Raleigh's grandmother would sign up. She lived here during the open months of April through November when she wasn't in Florida. "It's me. How are you, Stel?"

"I didn't know you'd be teaching this class. The confirmation letter had a woman's name on it." Stella hustled toward him for a big hug.

He returned it, of course. He'd always liked Raleigh's grandmother. She'd treated him well and had referred to him as her new favorite grandson. She'd accepted him as-is—the only one of them who'd done so.

"Teri went out early on maternity leave," Darren explained.

"Oh." Stella's gaze narrowed. "Bree! I didn't expect to see you here. Do you two know each other?"

"We just met." Bree smiled.

"Oh, well, good. That's good." Stella's penciled-in eyebrows arched toward her hairline. "How's your mom?"

"She needs to stay off her feet for a while, but she'll be fine."

"Fortunate for all of us. Yes, very fortunate." Stella glanced from him to Bree and then back to him. "Joan broke her ankle playing tennis. Can you imagine?"

There were worse things broken in life, but Darren didn't say that. He nodded as he watched more people enter the room. Mostly women, but a couple of men joined them, too. All of them looked well beyond retirement age. Could these people safely tromp around in the woods? He'd find out soon enough.

Bree listened to the DNR guy, Darren, introduce himself and explain the scope of the class. There were ten students, including her. She recognized several but didn't really know anyone except for Stella. They'd often shared a practice room back in the day when Stella played the violin. Bree had given her a few lessons and had loved their time together. What the woman lacked in skill, she more than made up for in flamboyant kindness.

Bree spotted the wire mesh basket in Stella's hands. Everyone else had a container or bag of sorts. The two men each had green net bags like the ones her avocados came in. All her mother had told her was that they'd meet here, go foraging and then come back to the community room for a quick demonstration on cleaning and preparing what they'd found. She hadn't considered bringing a container.

But then, that was a logical deduction and Bree wasn't exactly into logic. She believed people could change, when in reality they couldn't or wouldn't. Not to mention, she'd been told a thousand times that her head was too filled with notes and chords to return the milk to the fridge.

Bree scanned the paper calendar. She looked forward to today's hunt for black morels. Next week was ramps—whatever those were—and fiddlehead ferns. Her stomach turned at the last one. Memories of an argument over trying something as harmless as fiddlehead ferns rang through her thoughts. She should have ended it with Philip back then.

She zeroed in on wild asparagus in a class three weeks from now. She'd never realized her favorite vegetable could be found out in the wild. She'd assumed it was grown in gardens, having only purchased it in a grocery store.

Bree had never had a garden of her own. She wouldn't have begun to know what to do with one. Hours of daily practice on the cello had been a priority all her life. She'd missed out on a few things. Maybe a lot of things, but she wouldn't trade her music for anything. Or anyone. She'd realized that almost too late.

She wouldn't miss out today. This class promised something different than her usual routine. Right now, Bree craved different. For the first time in a long while, she felt free. Free to do whatever she wanted before following her dreams. A few weeks of relative leisure before the hard work began. Toiling under the tutelage of an orchestral composer for the next two years was a dream come true and one that would require all her focus.

"If no one has any questions about the paperwork, I'll collect it now, and then we can head out."

Bree snapped out of her thoughtful haze, helped gather up the signed waivers and handed them to Darren. "Here."

"Thank you." He gave her a tight nod, barely looking at her.

Bree couldn't help but look at him, though. His fingers were bare of any rings, and he had light brown hair that curled even though he kept it short. Despite the gray-green uniform he wore, she pictured him as a flannel shirt kind of guy. Like the lumberjack on those paper towel commercials. The breadth of Darren's shoulders hinted that he might not be a stranger to chopping wood.

Her pulse skittered when he caught her staring. His eyes were blue—bright blue and wary.

Bree smiled, hoping he understood that she meant no harm. She'd recently broken up with a man who'd nearly robbed her of her dreams. She wasn't about to risk another relationship that might trap her where she and her music had no place to grow.

"Let's load up." Darren made his way to the door as if he couldn't get out fast enough. Away from her.

Bree laughed under her breath. Was she scary? All she'd done was smile. Okay, maybe she'd checked him out thoroughly. But who'd blame her? He was a good-looking guy. Not that she'd do anything about it. She wasn't even window-shopping.

But if she were…

Another laughable thought. Still, Darren Zelinsky made for one very handsome display.

"Come on, honey. This is going to be fun." Stella patted her arm.

Bree had a feeling that might be true, but her curiosity had been piqued. "So, what's his story?"

"Darren?" Stella shook her head and whispered, "I'll tell you later. Come for dinner?"

Imaginings of a sordid, operatic tale tickled her curiosity. Bree wanted to know more. She leaned close. "I'd love to."

Stella wrapped her arm around Bree and squeezed. "You know my door's always open. Tonight we can cook up what we find."

Bree giggled. Something she did little of but always with Stella. "Sounds like a good plan."

"My plans are always good ones." Stella winked and headed out the door.

Bree dashed back into the kitchen for a couple of plastic storage bags to gather up those morel mushrooms. The last one finally to leave the building, she squinted at the sudden brightness outside. Three in the afternoon on the last Tuesday in April and the weather was perfect. The sun finally shone between puffy white clouds after a couple of days of gray rain.

Bree noted that everyone had already loaded up and waited for her to get in the van. Her stomach clenched. Did DNR Darren mind that she'd held them up? He didn't look too pleased.

The only seat left was the front passenger seat, next to him. She climbed in and glanced his way, but he was busy counting heads.

When he finished, she asked, "So, where are we going?"

"State land not far out of town." He didn't sound annoyed and concentrated on backing out.

Breathing easier, she asked more questions. "Do these black mushrooms grow out in the open?"

"In the woods."

"Oh." She glanced at her brand-new light gray flats and frowned.

Obviously she hadn't dressed right, but then, she wasn't an outdoorsy kind of gal. Her idea of a hike was walking the shoreline here or her parents' neighborhood in Royal Oak. It wasn't that she didn't like it outside, but living in Detroit didn't exactly invite running wild outdoors. She'd spent a lot of time inside practicing, where her imagination ran wild within the confines of a music room.

She noticed Darren's hands as he gripped the steering wheel. They were strong hands with scrapes and calluses. Nothing like the spotless manicured hands belonging to Philip. Darren was very different from the professionally polished man she'd dated far too long.

Another bomb she'd soon drop on her parents. She'd not only quit her position with the symphony to accept a music residency out west but also discarded her parents' chosen husband for her. The seemingly perfect man, but Bree knew better. He wasn't perfect for her.

The chatter and laughter behind them grew louder as they turned off a main road onto a dirt one. Bouncing along, Bree grabbed the handle on the door and glanced at Darren. His face looked carved out of stone. Obviously *he* wasn't having fun.

"Do you do this often?"

"What?"

"Give these kind of classes."

"This is my first." He drove slower and concentrated on the pathway ahead. He took another turn onto what couldn't really be called a road but had tracks proving vehicles had traveled it before.

Real chatty guy.

Bree bit her bottom lip and stared out the window. It was pretty here in the woods. The tender green leaves were just beginning to unfurl, way behind the spring growth downstate. She spotted a small tree with buds bursting into a white flower here and there. "What's that tree blooming over there?"

Darren looked where she pointed. "Juneberry tree."

"Oh."

"The fruit is edible."

"So, where'd you learn all this?"

Darren shrugged as he took another turn. "My grandmother taught me what to look for when I was a kid."

Bree melted when she thought of this big, gruff man as a small boy following his grandmother around, learning about wild food and where to find it. "Neat."

He grunted agreement, slowed the van to a stop and turned in his seat toward the passengers in the back. "After you get out, please stay near the van for instructions."

Amid grumbles from one of the elderly men, Bree peered through the windshield. They'd stopped in a small clearing surrounded by trees. The vehicle path went deeper into the woods, but evidently they were here, wherever here was. And it was bound to get interesting scouring the area with this group of rowdy seventy-year-olds.

Bree turned when she felt a pat on her shoulder. Looking into Stella's eyes, she chuckled when the elderly woman wiggled her eyebrows. As if she and Darren had hit it off. More like she'd made him angry, considering the way he barked orders.

She glanced at him, shocked to find him watching her. "What?"

"You getting out?"

Of course she was getting out. What did he think, after they'd come all this way she'd stay in the van? "Yes. Why?"

"No reason." He shrugged and exited the vehicle.

Bree watched him walk around the front. He tapped lightly on the hood as if dreading this. She knew irritation when she saw it. What was his problem, anyway?

Bree pocketed her phone and grabbed her bag. Maybe she should try to find out.

Chapter Two

Darren glanced at Bree as she slid from the passenger seat of the van, and he shook his head. She was dressed in light-colored cropped pants and shoes that were barely more than slippers. He'd be surprised if she stayed clean. Unless she was the prissy type that wouldn't get her hands dirty. She'd go home empty-handed if that were true.

She looked nothing like his ex-girlfriend, but Bree came from the same place. Overdressed for roaming around outside, she might as well have been cut from the same cloth as Raleigh.

He had ten people to look after. He needed to quit focusing on one. It was up to him to show them respect for the woods. And that meant staying alert. "Gather around, please."

Darren passed out plastic whistle lanyards to each person as they stepped close. "Stay in pairs at all times, and if you get turned around, just blow your whistle. I'll find you."

He waited for them to slip the whistles over their heads, and then he held up the wild edibles pamphlet. "Open your booklet to page three, and take a good look at the picture of the morel mushroom. Notice the pattern and the shape, with the bottom closed around the stem. That's what we're looking for. Stay away from the blobby-looking ones. They're false morels. There are also caps that are open on the bottom like an umbrella. They're edible, but use caution. They make some people sick. I'll go through what you find before we leave to make sure they're all safe. Any questions?"

Stella raised her hand.

"Stel?"

"We shouldn't eat them now, right?" She knew that but was trying to help him out.

He hadn't even thought about mentioning it and appreciated the reminder. These people didn't know what they were doing. This was a novelty. A vacation treat. "Right. They need to be cleaned of grit, and there might be a rare stowaway bug inside. Morels are way better cooked, in my opinion. I'll show you how to clean them when we return." He checked his watch. "Okay, we'll meet back here in forty-five minutes."

"Darren, will you find the first morel for us before we split up?" Stella asked.

He noticed everyone nodding in agreement. Okay, maybe he wasn't so good at leading this class. They had no clue what to look for and where. He'd almost sent them away without showing them. All because he'd been in a hurry to get rid of them. Especially Bree.

He gestured for them to follow and headed for a wooded area, keeping his gaze focused on the ground. "They're dark, a blackish-tan triangle. Look around these ash trees. See the gray bark?"

He noticed that Bree watched his every move and copied it. She bent down low but didn't touch anything. "Oh! Is this one?"

He leaned close to her, still bent over and staring at the ground. He could smell her perfume, or maybe it was her shampoo. Whatever it was, it stopped him cold like a sucker punch to the gut. The soft, flowery scent teased his senses and begged him to move closer.

He didn't.

He couldn't go there. Some things might smell good at first but ended up rotten. Spoiled rotten. He'd found that out much too late.

He took a knee and waited for the rest of the class to gather round. "This is exactly what we're looking for. Morels. Take care where you step and look around. Where there's one, there are bound to be more. Pinch off the stem so the roots stay in the ground. Like this."

He offered the mushroom to Bree.

"I get the first one?" Her fingertips grazed his palm as she scooped it up and dropped it into her plastic bag.

"You found it."

She grinned at him. Proud of herself.

Another sucker punch. The jaws of attraction snapped around him like a rusty old trap digging in deep. He couldn't let it poison his blood. Or his brain by giving it room to grow.

"Here are some!" one of the women announced, not far away.

Darren stopped staring at Bree and jogged over to inspect the finding. Sure enough, his class was on a roll as another morel was found, then another. "Good job. I think everyone's got it."

He pulled a small red onion bag from his pocket and joined the hunt.

"Why that kind of bag?" Bree came up from behind him. She had several mushrooms bulging from the bottom of her plastic grocery store variety.

"It lets the spores fall and reseed."

"Oh." She didn't wander far from his side.

Why'd she stick with him? He'd hoped she would have joined Stella's group of three ladies. He heard laughter and shouts as more found mushrooms, and Darren silently thanked the Lord for small favors. They hadn't been skunked on his first class.

"Should I pick these little ones?" Bree asked.

He stepped closer. They were small white morels yet to mature. "Go ahead. They'll get picked by somebody else if you leave 'em."

"So, people come way out here?"

He nodded. "A lot of people. I've run into campers from downstate, Ohio, even Indiana, up here picking on state land. Gather as much as they can to enjoy or sell."

"I've had morels before at a golf club dinner but never gave much thought to where they came from."

Local ingredients were desirable, and some of the finer restaurants in town paid top dollar to serve local morels. Darren didn't frequent those places anymore. The places Raleigh had dragged him to. Give him plain cooking at Dean's Hometown Grille in town any day. But his breakup had chased him from going there. Too many sympathy glances and gossip.

After Raleigh left him, Darren didn't go anywhere he might run into her. He'd stayed away from downtown Maple Springs, where she lived with his best friend, Tony. He'd stayed away from Bay Willows and the memories there, too. In fact, he pretty much stayed away from women in general. Too often they tried to turn him into someone he wasn't, like Raleigh had. She'd told him that he'd never change and was stuck in a rut doing the same thing all the time.

Maybe that was true, but Darren loved what he did. He'd grown up here, where the summer residents and tourists bloated the population from a mere two thousand to ten times that number, crowding out those who lived here year-round. Some of his friends had tried to emulate them in manner and dress. Tony had been one of them. Never content to embrace where he came from, Tony wanted more. Tony wanted too much and took more than he should have.

Darren glanced at Bree and spotted a mushroom at her feet. He bent to pluck it. If she wanted to know where morels came from, today's outing answered it. A person couldn't put a price tag on finding these. "They come from right here."

"I almost stepped on that one." She laughed and kept walking forward, slow and hunched over. Her hair fell like a curtain, draping her face from view. Her gray slip-ons were dirty at the toes, and her pants had streaks of dirt on them, too. She wore a gold-colored windbreaker that made her easy to spot. That color also made her eyes glow. Like a cat's eyes.

Darren wasn't real fond of cats. Even his parents' cat drove him nuts with all its hollering for attention, only to run away if he tried to pet it. Women were like cats in that way. He preferred dogs. Dogs didn't tease.

"Ooh, here's another couple." She picked them properly and foraged on, poking her fingers under dead leaves and raking through the clumps of grass here and there.

Well, she wasn't prissy. He'd give her that. He found a few more as well and checked his watch. Twenty minutes to go. He stood and glanced around the woods. Stella was out of sight, as were several others, but he heard lots of chatter. No one lost. That was good. Real good.

"So, what does a DNR officer do besides take a bunch of us resorters out in the woods to look for food?"

Resorters. Even that sounded pretentious.

"As a conservation officer," he corrected her, "my job is to provide natural resources protection and ensure recreational safety, as well as provide general law enforcement duties."

"That sounds like it came right out of a textbook."

"It did." Straight out of his employee handbook.

She smiled, causing those delectable dimples to reappear. "Do you like what you do?"

Here we go. The usual female digging. At first, Raleigh had liked the idea of what he did for a living—the whole man-in-uniform-with-a-gun thing. But then the limitations of his pay coupled with his desire to stay put in Northern Michigan had bothered her. Obviously too much. He should have believed her when she'd said she wanted to travel and eventually move away to a more urban area.

"I love my job." Darren didn't want to do anything else but grow within this region and climb the short ladder right here.

Bree nodded. "That's good."

Curious, he asked her the same. "What about you?"

"I play the cello."

The cello. That was the instrument whose name he couldn't remember. He stopped walking. "Hey, so that was you practicing before class."

Bree grinned. "It was. Along with a woman who plays the violin in a string quartet here. There are practice rooms above the community room. Bay Willows is hoping to start a summer music school. They've bought up a couple of vacant cottages near the community building, but I suppose you know that."

"I didn't." Something like that would only bring more people here. "You're good."

"I know." There was no bragging in her voice. She'd stated a simple fact. Like any professional acknowledging a skill level.

"Do you give lessons, then?"

She spotted another morel and picked it. "Not really. I'm not into teaching little kids how to play, you know? I play with the Detroit Symphony Orchestra—well, I used to."

"Used to?"

"I quit."

He stared at her. She obviously wanted him to ask the reason, and the funny thing was, Darren wanted to know. "Okay. Why?"

"Last year, I applied for a two-year music residency that would encompass composing. I'd like to compose. And, well, recently I got called and accepted." She let out a deep breath. "There, practice before delivery speech."

He didn't want to go there, but something about the vulnerable look in her eyes made him probe. "Is it a secret?"

"No. I've wanted to work under a composer for years, but I haven't ever had the chance before. My parents don't know yet, but then, it came together pretty fast."

She looked old enough to make her own decisions. "And they'll have a problem with it?"

Bree shrugged. There was obviously more to her story, but all she said was, "I'll find out."

He nodded and they fell silent, each one searching out mushrooms in opposite directions. After several minutes, he stood, stretched and spotted Bree a few yards away.

Her eyes were closed, her head tilted toward the sky. Her dark brown hair blazed with coppery color where the sun hit it.

His gut tightened. He didn't want to care about why this woman worried over her parents' reaction. He didn't want to like her at all, but there was something about her that tugged at him. Like a rare wildflower that needed protection from getting picked.

At that moment, she opened her eyes, looked right at

him and grinned. "I was listening to the sounds of the woods."

He cocked his head. What was she talking about?

"You know, the birdsong and the breeze rustling those crepe-paper-looking leaves on those little trees over there." She wasn't putting him on.

"I can't remember what they are. Some kind of aspen, maybe." He wished he knew. He'd look it up.

"Interesting sounds out here."

"Haven't you been in the woods before?"

"I've summered here most of my life, but I've never ventured far from the main thoroughfares. Maybe Traverse City or Mackinac Island."

He shook his head. "You're missing the best parts of Northern Michigan."

She turned interested eyes on him. "So, where are these best parts?"

He took the bait. "Open fields with hills rising behind them. A twisting river loaded with brookies. The Pigeon River Forest where elk roam. Come winter, there are awesome snowmobile trails, pine trees heavy with snow and blue moonlight."

She gave him an odd look. "You sound like a poet."

Darren kicked at the ground cover. He'd gotten carried away. "I appreciate the area, is all."

"No desire to live elsewhere?"

"None." He was a local. He'd always be a local even though he'd been an army baby. His mother had moved him and his brother Zach permanently to Maple Springs after their brother Cam was born. She'd wanted her kids to have a home, an anchor. Some of his siblings had flown far from the nest after high school, but Darren wasn't a traveler. He'd gone to college only a couple hours away before attending conservation officer training academy.

The people who summered at Bay Willows came from all over. Mainly the Midwest, sure, but most were well-traveled and liked to tell where they'd been. They peppered their conversation with travel itineraries the way folks in old movies plastered travel stickers on their suitcases. Raleigh used to tease that he was backward, having never really been anywhere as an adult.

"Hmm." Bree's attention zeroed in on the ground. "Oh, here are some more."

Glad for the distraction, Darren let the matter drop, because it didn't matter. Bree Anderson was both educated and no doubt well-traveled. She was accustomed to a lifestyle he'd never had and never would have. With the supervisor position came a pay increase that would be more than enough for him. He didn't care about making scads of money.

If Bree found him interesting, it was only temporary. He wasn't the kind of guy a girl like Bree would keep for the long haul. Darren wasn't good enough for the Bay Willows crowd. He'd learned that lesson pretty well. Darren only had to make a mistake once to know he'd never repeat it.

On the drive back to Maple Springs, Bree peered into her plastic grocery sack at the pile of blackish-tan edibles heaped there. She breathed in the soft, earthy smell of fungi. Nothing too strong or pungent, she had trouble coming up with a comparison for the aroma. She'd picked these delicacies in the woods, with her own two hands.

How cool.

"How many do you have?" Darren's voice sounded awfully gentle for such a gruff guy.

"Uh." Bree looked up. She sat up front again, in the passenger seat. "I don't know."

Darren's mouth curved into a half smile. "Considering

how long you were staring into that bag, I thought you were counting them."

"Nope, just smelling them." She didn't want to explain what a novel experience this had been for her. Different than what she was used to and, well, it had been fun. Really fun. But more importantly, it had made her feel strong. Capable. Empowered?

Okay, maybe that went too far.

He chuckled, the sound a soft rumble from within his chest. Maybe he wasn't as gruff as he pretended to be.

Bree's phone whistled with an incoming text, and she pulled it from her coat pocket. Briefly she closed her eyes after she'd read the name. That made three this week. "Excuse me."

"No problem."

Call me when you get a chance. Want to see how you're doing. Philip.

Bree had no intention of calling him. Instead, she replied with a text.

I'm fine. Helping with one of my mom's classes. Thanks.

She scanned two previous messages that were similar. One had been Philip checking that she'd made it safely to her parents' summer cottage. She was okay with that one, but the next two? Really, Philip needed to let it go. He needed to let *her* go.

Bree slipped the phone back into her pocket as the van pulled up to the community building. Clutching her cache of mushrooms, she got out with the rest of the group and headed inside.

"Gather in the kitchen and I'll show you how to clean and cook the morels," Darren called.

"I know how to cook mushrooms." The grumbly guy named Ed had a decidedly sharp tone.

Bree glanced at Darren. He looked calm enough despite the flush of red that tipped his ears.

"We all do. In fact, you can prepare morels any way you'd normally cook or sauté other mushrooms. Personally, I like to bread mine. It's no problem if you prefer not to stick around."

Bree looked back at Ed.

The old guy wasn't appeased by Darren's offer to leave. "Now look here—"

"I'd like to know how you cook them," Bree quickly interrupted.

Others agreed. Situation diffused.

Bree relaxed as the tension eased and Ed nodded for Darren to continue. As if he was somehow in charge.

Darren had been beyond patient when they'd run late because there were so many mushrooms to find and pick. No one had wanted to leave. Including Bree. Who'd have guessed she'd enjoy roaming the woods so much? She didn't even care that her shoes were dirty or her pants filthy from wiping her fingers on them.

Darren showed that same patience now in the face of Ed's belligerence as he emptied his morels into a bowl in the sink. "Cleaning is easy. Just soak them in salt water, swish them around a bit, and then rinse and drain like so. Get as much water off as you can. Then you're ready to cook."

Bree watched as he laid the washed mushrooms out on paper towels. And the questions started to fly.

"Can you dry them for storing?"

"Yes."

"How?"

"String them up to air-dry or use the lowest setting on a dehydrator. I've seen them laid out on an old window screen in the sun to dry."

That got their class buzzing with chatter.

"What about freezing?" another asked.

"Freeze after drying, or freeze after sautéing. If you freeze after picking, don't wash them. If they're wet you'll ruin them."

Bree nearly laughed at Darren's clipped answers. He looked like a man who wanted out of there. His earlier patience had worn thin. She watched as he quickly melted a huge glob of butter in a frying pan before dredging the mushrooms in a flour mixture. He threw the coated morels in the pan.

The group murmured likes and dislikes while the intoxicating smell of melted butter and sizzling mushrooms teased Bree's senses. Her stomach grumbled in response.

"Not good for my diet," one of the ladies said.

Several agreed. But Bree didn't care. Those things looked and smelled delicious.

"What's that mixture you use?" Ed sounded almost polite. Not quite, but still.

Darren took his time answering, turning the morels over in the pan. "Flour, salt and pepper. Seasoned salt works, too."

Bree scanned their group huddled around the island waiting as Darren ladled those butter-fried mushrooms onto a paper towel–lined plate.

He lifted the plate to share. "Be careful. They're hot."

In this batch, there were enough mushrooms for everyone to try a couple. Bree waited till the end before she took her two. The anticipation was worth it. She closed her eyes while savoring the buttery, mild mushroom taste.

"Well?" He tipped his head. Did he really want to know what she thought?

Bree soaked his interest up like a sponge. "Firm texture and subtle flavor. These are really good."

Darren smiled. Big and broad like his shoulders.

And Bree was momentarily stunned. At a loss for words, all because of one smile from one interesting, burly man sharing a moment, an actual connection with her—over cooked mushrooms!

She popped the last morel into her mouth and mumbled, "I've got to run."

Class wrapped up quickly after Bree scurried out. She reminded him of his sisters who'd up and bolt when they'd suddenly remember they left their curling irons plugged in somewhere. But surely that couldn't be it. Bree's hair was straight and shiny. Would that thick mass of mink-colored tresses be soft or coarse to the touch?

He scowled. Not the kind of thoughts he should have.

"What? Did you find some grease that we missed?" Stella and a couple other women had helped him clean up in minutes.

"No. No. It's nothing." He gave them a nod. "Thank you, ladies. Next week, same time and place."

"See you then." Stella walked away and then turned back. "You did a great job today, Darren. Thank you."

Warmth filled him, mixed with shame at spurning her concern this past year. "You're welcome. Good to see you again, Stel."

"And you, as well." She winked and left with her small entourage of elderly friends.

Darren could count on her for good buzz on his class. Maybe this time around, his regional boss would see that he was ready to deal with anyone. Even the Bay Willows crowd.

When he climbed into the van, he blew out his breath. *Not bad.* His first wild edibles class was done, along with today's shift. And he hadn't run into any problems or his ex. All that stressing over nothing. He'd have to face her one of these days, but not today.

Starting the engine, he checked his rearview mirror, caught a glimpse of a pink-and-green-striped bag on one of the seats and groaned. His day wasn't over yet. He'd have to return that purse to the owner.

He reached back and grabbed it. Hesitating only a moment, he looked inside. Rifling through a woman's purse was not something he relished, but after digging around lipstick tubes and travel packs of tissues, he found a wallet. As he opened that, a driver's license with a picture of Stella greeted him.

At least he knew where she lived. He'd been there many times, with and without Raleigh. He used to stop in to fix a thing or two around Stella's cottage. Who took care of that now? Tony? He doubted that. Tony wasn't exactly a fix-it kind of guy. He'd call a repair man with the excuse that he had more money than time.

Tony knew all about money. From the world of high finance and investments, his best friend had spoken Raleigh's language far better than Darren ever had. The sting of their betrayal still lingered. It wasn't easy to lose his bride and best man in one day—one horrible day that had changed everything.

He pulled into the small driveway of Stella's cottage with the screened-in porch and looked around. No cars were parked nearby other than Stella's little black Buick. He stepped onto the porch. Crisp white wicker furniture with brightly colored cushions had been casually arranged.

A vase stuffed with tall, fake flowers stood sentinel on the glass-topped side table.

And this was only the porch.

He finally knocked on the door.

"Darren, what a nice surprise." Stella wore a red-and-white-checkered apron, looking very much like anyone's grandma, only a lot brighter. She applied more makeup than most. "Come in."

He lifted her purse. "I'm just dropping this off. You left it in the van."

"Oh, my. I didn't even miss it. Don't get old." She opened the screen door wide and it squeaked. The thing needed a good dousing of lubricant on the hinges. "Come in for a bit, would you?"

He'd fix the door before he left. Giving Stella a nod he said, "You're not old."

"Thanks, but we both know I am."

He followed Stella into the small summer cottage. She lived alone. Raleigh once said that her husband had died only a couple of years ago.

A lot had happened in those two years. Darren had lost out on his bid for the supervisor position, and then he'd met Stella's granddaughter. It had been a whirlwind romance, one that Darren reeled from still. Memories sliced through him as he walked past the dining room into Stella's kitchen. He could almost hear Raleigh's laughter and the way she'd teased.

It hurt.

"Cookies? I made them this morning."

Darren sat down with a sigh. "Sure."

She patted his shoulder. "How are you?"

"I'm okay." Broken hearts mended with time but never forgot.

"Have you talked to Raleigh?" Stella bustled about the

kitchen, stacking cookies on a plate and then pouring him a tall glass of milk.

"Not much to say, is there?"

Stella gave him a long look. "I suppose not."

The question he didn't want to ask nagged like a loose tooth until he finally spit it out. "Is she happy?"

Stella nodded. "She appears to be. Tony's always buying her stuff. His last gift was a diamond ring."

Darren clenched his jaw. He hadn't seen them in months. Nineteen months, three weeks and a few days, to be exact.

She stared him down with a fierce gleam in her eyes. "You're a good man, Darren. Much too good for my granddaughter."

That surprised him, and he grunted around a mouthful of chocolate chip cookie. Stella's granddaughter had stormed into his life and changed it. He'd forever be the spurned groom nearly left at the altar when his bride ran away with his best man after rehearsal. They'd taken off for the honeymoon and had the gall to come back and live under Darren's nose in town. Was it any wonder that people in town looked at him with pity?

He drained his glass and slammed it down on the table. Fortunately, he didn't break the thing, but the loud thwack startled Stella.

He stood. "I'll fix that squeak in your screen door."

Stella smiled up at him. "Do that and I'll make you dinner. I was thinking chicken marsala with those morels we picked. Stay and eat with me."

He looked into her eager face. A few more wrinkles creased around Stella's blue eyes since the last time he'd seen her. For a woman in her early seventies, she was spry. Energetic and a good listener. She'd always been a good listener. Dinner might be a little earlier than he was used to, but food sounded good right now. What harm could there be in staying?

"Okay. I'll stay, on one condition."

"What's that?"

"What else needs fixing around here?"

Stella grinned, obviously pleased. "Well, there is a leaky faucet upstairs."

"Now we're talking." Darren knew where the tools were kept and got to work rummaging for what he'd need. Really, he should have stopped in and checked on Stella sooner.

He could hear her humming while she scattered pots and pans in the kitchen. The phone rang. Stella still had a landline.

"Yup, now's good." Stella's voice dropped to a whisper.

He headed up the stairs so he wouldn't overhear her private conversation. Halfway up, it dawned on him that Stella might be talking to her granddaughter and his gut twisted. Surely, Stella had enough sense not to invite Raleigh over while he was here. He backed down a few steps and strained to listen, but Stella had already hung up the phone.

She was humming again.

Chapter Three

"How was class? Was there a good turnout?" Bree's mother sat on the couch, her broken ankle propped up on a pillow. She wore a soft cast-style boot and had instructions to keep weight off it as much as possible for the next week.

Bree slipped into a pair of loose loafers to match the khakis she'd changed into. "It was good. Including me, there were ten of us. Stella was there."

"How is she?"

"Good. I'm heading over there for dinner."

Her mother frowned. "We've hardly had a chance to talk since you came up. Everything okay?"

Bree hesitated. Really, she was making too much of telling her parents about Philip. About her leaving. "Everything's good. Really good. In fact, I was offered that residency I applied for."

"In Seattle?" Aha, her mother had been paying attention all those months ago. "I thought they chose someone else."

"They did, but something came up and the guy had to decline. I gave notice to the symphony, cleaned out my apartment and shipped out what I'll need. I'll leave here in about a month."

Her mother narrowed her gaze. "What's Philip think about that?"

This was where it got sticky. "We decided to call it quits. It's for the best, all things considered."

"Oh, Bree. He's got a wonderful future ahead of him. You're twenty-nine years old. Isn't it time you stopped studying and settled down?"

Bree had expected that reaction. She'd gone for her master's degree and a couple of short-term fellowships overseas while working her way up to assistant principal cellist. She wasn't ready to get stuck with kids and a husband who'd make demands on her time. She needed to find her real purpose before settling down. Why had she been gifted with the love of music if simply playing was not enough?

Her parents had introduced her to Philip, the son of her father's golf buddy, years ago, with high hopes. Hopes that Bree had shared until she'd applied for the music residency. Philip had been against it from the start, vocalizing that she didn't have a chance. He'd been livid when she went ahead with her application anyway.

She shrugged, sparing her mother the details. "It just didn't work out between us."

"He doesn't want to wait. Two years is a long time, Bree. Maybe you should rethink this residency."

Bree breathed deep. "I've always wanted to try my hand at composing, and this is a prime opportunity."

Her mother didn't understand her restlessness. She'd never understood her desire to be more. Instead of arguing the point, her mother shelved the discussion for later, when she'd have reinforcement from Bree's father. "Well, it's good to have you here for longer than a couple of weeks. You might even catch your sister. She's finally taking some time off and will be up Memorial Day weekend."

Bree bit her lip. Her sister had been the role model in the family. She was a dermatologist married to a doctor with two kids. It didn't get more successful than that in her mother's eyes. "That's great."

Her mother tipped her head. "Thank you for overseeing my class. How'd that officer do? He's filling in, you know. The woman I met with was supposed to facilitate but went out early on maternity leave. And no wonder, considering she's got to be in her forties. See, that could happen to you if you wait too long to have kids. It's a risk, Bree."

She didn't bother addressing that issue. She had plenty of time. Even if she didn't, she'd never been comfortable around small children and wasn't sure she even wanted a family of her own. "So, you haven't met him."

"No. Someone called to tell me about the change a week ago. And then this happened." Her mom lifted her ankle.

"He did a great job. He's knowledgeable." Bree didn't mention that Darren was also attractive and single. Or that Ed had given him grief.

"Well, good. If it's successful, we might offer this class every year."

"I think that's a good idea." Would Darren teach it? If so, she'd be sorry to miss it.

Bree definitely thought this class more fun than most of the interest offerings available through the summer season at Bay Willows. Pottery, painting and bridge were only a few. Her mother, as president of the garden club, had organized the wild edibles course months ago.

"Well, I've got to run. Stella had just started making dinner when I called her. I left a bowl of cleaned morels in the fridge for you and Dad."

"Your father will enjoy them."

She'd split half her bundle with her parents; the other half was going with her. A convenient escape for tonight, but her mother was bound to tell her father the news, and then they'd both sit her down for more information.

Her father would want to know what kind of living she could expect over the next two years. Bree had cashed in her 401(k) to handle incidentals, plus she had a good savings. Room and board were covered in a dorm-like setting as there were other residents working in other areas, but that was pretty much it when it came to compensation.

She had a little over a month up north where troubles melted away in the deep blue waters of Lake Michigan. Only she'd be gone before the lake was warm enough for swimming.

Bree took a deep breath and then let it back out. "Is there anything you need before I go?"

Her mother stared over the rim of her reading glasses and lifted her needlepoint. "I've got this to keep me busy, and your father's outside. I'll be fine."

Her father would be around all week before heading back home to his job in Detroit. He'd make the four and a half-hour trek north to the cottage every weekend, though. Bree had grown up that way. Seeing her father only on weekends during the summer months.

Bree headed out the door. From the front porch, she scanned the gorgeous view of Maple Bay and sighed. The dark blue waters of Lake Michigan slapped rhythmically against the shore while birds sang their hearts out. If only she could capture these sounds and turn them into chords and notes. The view always inspired a chorus in her head. Could sight somehow be translated into sound? A good composer used all the senses.

Could she be good?

She'd written oodles of movements with the hope of putting it all together. One day, she'd hear her own piece played. If she was successful in her residency, others would hear it, too, and she'd finally prove herself capable of not only playing but also creating good string music. She'd rise above the title of simple musician to something special. A real artist.

Bree walked the short couple of blocks away from the shoreline to Stella's cottage, set back against the wooded area. Her stomach dipped when she spotted a big green passenger van with the DNR emblem on the doors. Darren stood on the porch, opening and closing the screen door. Then he went inside.

Bree bit her lip. Maybe he'd only stopped by. And maybe she was acting like a kid with a school yard crush, suddenly afraid to talk to the man. Good grief, she'd see him next week at class and the week after, so what was the big deal?

He was the big deal. Big and strong and attractive, Darren fell on the other side of the bell curve compared to the men she knew. Not that she'd dated all that much before Philip, but she was used to musicians, not strapping outdoorsmen with a chip a mile wide on their broad shoulders.

Walking forward, Bree stepped up onto the screened porch and rapped on the door, then opened it. "Hello?"

Stella hustled down the hallway and waved her in. "Come in the kitchen and you can help me finish dinner."

Bree heard the sound of water running from upstairs followed by a clinking of metal against metal. Then the running faucet again.

"Darren's fixing a couple of things for me. And he's staying for dinner."

"Oh, then I don't want to intrude." Bree backed up a step or two.

"Nonsense." Stella dropped her voice to a whisper. "I purposely left my purse behind so he'd have to stop by. I wanted you two to get to know each other better."

"Stella…" Bree followed her friend into the kitchen.

"Oh, come on. Have a little fun." Stella wiggled her overly penciled eyebrows. "He could use a little female attention."

"Oh? And why is that?" Bree couldn't imagine Darren having any trouble getting a date.

"Broken engagement with my granddaughter. She did the breaking." Stella pursed her lips, obviously not pleased.

"Oh, wow. Darren and Raleigh?" Bree had heard rumors a couple of summers ago about another man. She didn't know Darren was the one who'd been jilted. Betrayed.

Stella nodded. "Be nice to him. That's all I'm saying."

"Stella!" Bree felt for the guy. She really did. It made perfect sense that he'd avoided her. Well, Darren didn't have to worry. Bree had broken it off with Philip because he'd made her choose between him and her music. She couldn't risk another romantic entanglement. No way.

Stella handed her a small cutting board. "He's a good man."

"I'm sure he is—"

"You cut up the morels," Stella interrupted. "I'll get to work on the marsala."

"Okay." She was glad she'd changed topics. Bree knew her way around Stella's kitchen and grabbed a knife. She got to work slicing the rinsed mushrooms, then moved on to making a salad while Stella finished the chicken.

Her thoughts were tied up, trying to remember what she'd heard about Stella's granddaughter. Bree recalled there had been some sort of scandal, something her mother had once said, but Bree hadn't ever paid much attention to the Bay Willows grapevine. Too much fodder to take in.

Footsteps sounded on the wide plank floors, and Bree looked up.

"That smells awe-sssome—" Darren's voice fell away to nothing when he spotted her and frowned.

"Hello." Bree gave him a sheepish smile, feeling like she'd been caught with her hands in the cookie jar—knowing about him and Raleigh.

"Hey."

The wild rabbits that ran around Bay Willows looked less twitchy than this man seeing her here.

"Darren, watch the chicken a minute, would you, while I set the dining room table." Stella exited fast with an arm load of things from the fridge. She was more than a little obvious in leaving them alone.

Bree's cheeks flushed red-hot. "I'm sorry. She invited me, too."

"Nothing to apologize for." Darren stepped close to the stove and stirred the sauce. He turned down the heat. "I hadn't planned to stay, and—"

Horrified, Bree blurted, "You're not going to leave because of me, are you?"

He tipped his head and gave her a cool stare. "What I was going to say is that Stella twisted my arm with the promise of dinner if I fixed the faucet upstairs. Stella's a good cook."

"Oh." Bree relaxed. Sort of. "Sorry."

"Stop saying you're sorry."

"Sorr—I mean, okay." Then she laughed. "It's a habit."

"Saying you're sorry?" Darren didn't look amused by that.

"When I'm nervous, yes." Bree's stomach dropped again. That was a stupid thing to say, but she was used to apologizing to Philip in order to stop an argument before it started.

Darren chuckled. "*You're* nervous?"

Yes. Because you're way too attractive.

Instead of admitting that, Bree squared her shoulders. "Wrong choice of words, perhaps, but I feel like maybe I'm imposing."

"Trust me, you're not."

Silence settled thick between them until he looked around. "Stella? I think it's ready."

"Good. Turn off the heat and put the lid on it." Stella entered the kitchen and foraged in the fridge once more. "What do you two want to drink?"

"Water's fine," Bree said as she ducked out with the salad bowl and set it on the dining room table.

"Same for me." Darren's deep voice sounded a little too loud.

"You're both boring," Stella chirped as she handed over a pitcher of ice-cold water from the fridge. "Now go sit down. I'll bring out the chicken."

Bree remained in the dining room, waiting.

Darren entered and sat down right across from her, leaving the chair at the head of the table for their host. He looked at her.

She looked back.

Be nice to him. Stella's words roused a nervous laugh Bree choked off before it bubbled out. Darren didn't look like he wanted *nice*. Or anything to do with her, for that matter.

Stella set a large covered dish in the middle of the table. Fragrant steam leaked out, teasing Bree's appetite and stealing her attention.

"Darren, would you mind saying the blessing?" Stella bowed her head.

"Sure." Darren bowed his, too.

Bree followed suit, curious to hear the man pray.

"Bless us, O Lord, and these, Thy gifts, which we are

about to receive from Thy bounty. Through Christ, our Lord. Amen."

"Amen," Stella echoed.

Bree glanced at Darren. Did he truly believe? A rote prayer wasn't exactly a blazing emblem of faith, but then she wasn't exactly the pillar of piety, either. Having only come to salvation through Christ recently, Bree had her moments. She was often wrapped up in her own way instead of seeking God's will for her life. But not when it came to her upcoming residency. That was an opportunity, a gift she wouldn't squander.

Darren caught her staring at him and raised his eyebrows in question along with a bowl. "Salad?"

"Yes, please."

"So, Bree, tell us what you've been up to. Darren, did you know she plays the cello?" Stella scooped steaming chicken and sauce-drenched pasta onto her plate. "She used to give me lessons when I played the violin."

Bree smiled. "Say the word and I will again."

Stella patted her hand. "You'd make a great teacher, my dear."

She shook her head. "With adults maybe, but I don't have the patience for kids or beginners."

Darren gave her a nod. "I overheard her play just before class. She's good."

"I'm heading to Seattle at the beginning of June for a two-year residency with a symphony out there. We'll find out if I'm any good at composing."

Stella's eyes widened. "Really? I had no idea. Joan never mentioned anything."

"She didn't know. I just found out, too. I landed this opportunity only because the initial person chosen had a family situation and declined."

"Well, congratulations." Stella smiled.

Bree smiled back. "I'm excited about it."

Darren visibly relaxed. "Two years, huh? Then what?"

Bree shrugged. "I'll find out then. I hope. Working under a composer is something I've dreamed of doing since college. It's really a gift from God."

Darren nodded. "He does that."

That sure sounded like a man of faith talking. "I figured a month up here before leaving might be a good thing. A gift to myself before the hard work begins. Have some fun, you know? Instead of practice, practice, practice."

"Good for you," Stella said.

Bree looked at Darren. "I really enjoyed today's class, by the way. I've never gone off the beaten path into the woods like that. I'm already psyched for next week, looking for fiddleheads."

Darren glanced at Stella.

"See, I told you it was good," Stella said.

Darren shrugged, but those bright blue eyes of his studied Bree. "There's much more than just woods to explore up here."

He'd said that before. "Like blue moonlight?"

"I could show you around some." He looked surprised by his offer.

She was, too, and glanced at Stella.

Be nice to him.

Stella gave her a confident nod, grinning a little too widely. "He knows this area like the back of his hand. You'll be safe, dear, that's for sure."

Safe.

Bree appreciated safety. Knowing Darren was a man of faith and leery of "female attention," as Stella put it, reassured that his offer was not a come-on. DNR Darren wasn't looking for a romantic replacement. Even if he was, Bree already had a position lined up that would take all her energy.

One she wouldn't miss for the world.

Maybe seeing the countryside would inspire her. Something to look back on when things got hard. An intense music residency was bound to get hard, and Bree might need all the inspiration she could get while locked inside for hours on end. Could hanging out with Darren help in some way? After today's outing, she knew it'd be fun.

"You know what? I'll take you up on that offer." Bree nearly laughed at the brief flash of fear that shone from his eyes.

For a split second, Darren looked like he'd jumped in before measuring the depth of a cold lake.

He was handsome, sure, but he had nothing to fear from her. She was safe, too.

Darren couldn't believe he'd just asked this woman out. Maybe not in the conventional sense, but offering to show her what lay off the beaten path might as well have been a date. His grandmother called it courting. He nearly laughed at the thought. He wasn't the get dressed up and bring flowers kind of guy like his grandmother's description of the ideal date. Darren didn't dress up for anyone. Still, Bree surprised him by agreeing to go. He couldn't exactly backpedal his way out of this one without looking like an idiot.

"Where will you take her first?" Stella asked innocently enough, but there was a determined gleam in her eye. She was barking up the wrong tree if she thought to play matchmaker. Hadn't Stella heard? Bree would be gone in a month's time. Gone for two years.

"Not sure." He stalled, and then it dawned on him. "I'm going smelt dipping Friday night with friends. You could come with me."

"What's smelt dipping?" Bree's pretty brow furrowed. Everything about her was pretty. Even the measured way she ate her food was pretty, making sure her pasta was well covered in sauce before taking a bite. She didn't hurry. Refined and polite, she ate slowly.

What would she think about the robust way his family wolfed down a meal? Growing up with six brothers and three sisters, all younger but one, he'd learned to grab food quickly—shovel it in and then go back for seconds before the food was wiped out. Not that Bree would ever meet his family, much less have dinner with them.

Chances were good that if Bree went smelt dipping, she wouldn't like it. Then she might not want to go anywhere else. He'd fulfill his sightseeing offer and that'd be the end of it.

He leaned back in his chair, finished with his dinner. "Smelt are small fish we catch at night with nets. They run into rivers this time of year to spawn."

Bree wrinkled her nose. "I've never fished before."

Genius! He really was a genius at times. He could tell by the pinched look on her face that she wouldn't like it. "It's not real fishing. Not like with a pole, but it's still a good time."

"Hmm. When?"

"We're meeting at the river's edge at nine o'clock, Friday night." He waited for Bree to pass on this opportunity. From her expression, he knew she wasn't interested.

"I'll give it a try."

That answer threw him. She must be serious about trying new things. Only Darren didn't want to be one of those new things. It wasn't as though Bree flirted. Every time he'd looked at her, she'd looked away. And she wasn't shy. Bree had talked her fair share over dinner.

"So, where is this river?"

He glanced at Stella, and it dawned on him that it'd waste time for him to backtrack into town to pick up Bree. He didn't want her getting lost on the way, either, driving by herself. "It's north, nearly to Mackinaw City. We could meet somewhere in between."

Stella paused in sopping up the last of her marsala sauce with a crust of bread. "Why don't you two meet at your house? It's not hard to find and on the way."

Stella had been to his house with Raleigh only once, and yet she remembered the location. Her suggestion made sense, but something about Bree in his home made him squirm.

Bree didn't appear bothered by any of it. She waited for him to respond like it didn't matter to her one way or another. Bree was moving away in a month. Far away, too. Of course it didn't matter where she met him. She wasn't interested in him. He was crazy to think she'd be interested in hanging out with him for some temporary connection before leaving.

"Do you have a piece of paper?" he finally asked.

Stella jumped up and grabbed a notepad and pen, handing it over with a victorious grin.

Darren looked at Bree. She'd finished the last of her salad and then drained her water glass. When she wiped her full-lipped mouth with a napkin, he swallowed hard. A lot could happen in a month.

He concentrated on the paper. "I'll draw you a map. I'm right off the main road, but back in the woods a few miles."

"Okay." Bree tipped her head and watched him. She listened close as he explained when and where to look for his turn off.

He handed her the paper. "My cell is listed there, too."

"Looks easy enough. Thanks." Bree reached across and took the pen, then scribbled a number down and ripped it off. "Here's my number, just in case something comes up between now and then."

Darren pocketed the note and stood with plate in hand. "Stel, I'm going to take off."

"Thanks for fixing my faucet." Stella took the plate from him. "And you don't need to clean up, I got it."

"Thanks for dinner." Then he faced Bree. "See you Friday."

"Friday. I'll meet you at your place by eight-fifteen." She sounded so professional, like they'd scheduled a business meeting. Not a date.

"Sounds good." Ignoring the twist in his gut, Darren justified showing Bree around as an extension of his job.

A good word from Bree or her mom into the right ears might go a long way in upping his chances for the supervisor position. He'd take all the help he could to make sure he got the job this time.

He'd simply showcase the great up north outdoors and be done with it. When Bree left, he'd be done with her, too.

Chapter Four

By Friday night, the weather had turned chilly, so Bree dressed in warm layers. Who knew how long they'd be outside? Her parents thought she was crazy to venture out so late. Maybe they were right.

Following the map Darren had drawn was easy. She'd driven on the one main road heading north most of the way. Slowing down, she spotted the Honey for Sale sign right where he'd said it would be. Bree took the next right onto a dirt road. So far, so good.

Scanning the map again, she went another two miles until she saw the fish mailbox. This was Darren's driveway. It was a dirt two-track path similar to the ones they'd taken to find mushrooms. She slowed to a stop and stared at that mailbox.

What was she doing coming here?

With a deep breath, she squared her shoulders and pulled into the two-mile drive. No regrets. No missed opportunities.

Her cell phone buzzed with an incoming text. She slowed to a stop and grabbed it, hoping it wasn't Darren changing their plans. Another text from Philip that she ignored.

Darren hadn't been kidding when he said he lived in the woods. She'd watched the sun dip low in the sky as she drove here, but the surrounding trees with new leaves blocked the dwindling light.

When she finally pulled into a large clearing, the wood home surprised her. She'd expected something far less airy than the chalet-style structure in front of her. Darren's home was small but pretty with a wraparound deck that was partly covered and sat atop a two-bay garage. Another metal garage stood nearby.

She smiled when she saw him outside with two small beagles. Both were brown and white with black backs, floppy ears and sweet faces. Darren hunched down to give them each a pat and scratch behind their ears. Tails wagging, they followed him around a fenced area begging for attention. He gave in and petted them some more.

Stella had assured her that Darren was a good guy, but the gentle way he treated his dogs proved it.

She parked her car, got out and looked around. Wood stacked neatly under an overhang between the garage and stairway caught her eye. An axe lay against a beam with more wood scattered on the ground. She'd been spot-on with her lumberjack comparison. He even wore a padded flannel shirt.

"Hey." He gave her a cautious smile. "You're early."

Only fifteen minutes early. She walked toward the fenced dog run. "I gave myself extra time in case I got lost. Your dogs are adorable. What are their names?"

Darren stood facing her on the other side of the fence. "Mickey and Clara."

"Hi, guys." Bree stuck her fingers through the fence, and both dogs jostled to lick her hand in greeting. "Do they stay outside?"

"When I'm working. They have access to part of the garage so they can get out of the weather."

She nodded. "You have a nice home."

He looked surprised by her compliment. "Thanks. It's a prefab, but I've added a few things. The deck is one of them. I need to gather some gear, and then we can go. What size shoe do you wear?"

"Seven and a half. Why?"

"I have a pair of waders that might fit you. Come in and try them on."

"Weighters?" Bree followed him through the open garage door into a spotless space without a single vehicle parked inside. The walls had shelves filled with all sorts of outdoor gear—fishing poles, snowshoes. She pointed to a big metal safe. "What's that?"

"Waders? They're pull-on overall boots to wade into the water."

"No, that big green thing in the corner."

"Gun cabinet."

She felt her eyes widen at the size of the thing. "You have a lot of guns."

He laughed. "I have firearms for both work and recreation. So, yeah. I have a few."

Her stomach tightened. She didn't know men with guns. Philip's anger over her residency had unsettled her big-time. It was the reason she finally broke it off with him. What would a big guy like Darren turn into when he was mad? Stella's assurance that he was safe shriveled to nothing in the presence of that green cabinet.

She spotted a deer head mounted on the opposite wall and wrinkled her nose. "So, you hunt, too."

"Yup." His eyes challenged her to make something of it. "I like to fill my freezer."

"Oh." Of course, he killed his own food. Who was she

to raise an eyebrow? She ate meat with no thought to where it came from. Just like the morels.

"Have you ever tried venison?" His voice sounded softer now. More coaxing.

"No." She heard the whine of the dogs. They were inside the other garage bay that had been fenced off and poked their noses through the wire.

"It's good."

"Hmm. Maybe." She wrinkled her nose.

Darren laughed. "There are no maybes about it."

Bree ambled over to the dogs and gave them each a pat over the low fence, noticing their inside space looked pretty comfy. They had their own couch, water bowls and a basket of chew toys. This man took good care of his pets.

"Here, try these on. You'll stay warmer in these." He held out a pair of tan overalls with boots. *Waders.*

"So, you go into the water to catch these things?"

"You can net from shore, but that's not nearly as fun."

Bree was here to have fun, no matter how cold the thought of getting into a river at the end of April. She took the waders, found a chair to sit on and slipped off her sneakers. She'd never expected to do this sort of thing, so she hadn't brought any kind of boots with her up north. They'd already been shipped out to Seattle. Not that she owned a pair of real hiking boots. Maybe she'd buy a pair. She had a feeling trekking off the beaten path with Darren might be rough in spots.

She shoved one foot in, then the other, and stood.

"Walk a little. How do they feel?"

She galumphed her way around. "Big."

"I've got heavy socks upstairs. Come on."

She slipped out of the waders and followed him in her stocking feet, leaving her sneakers on the floor. She wanted a peek at the inside of his house. That said a lot about a man, didn't it? Too bad she hadn't paid attention to Philip's showy high-rise apartment.

Stepping onto the main floor, she was far from enlightened other than another deer head mounted over the fireplace and some fish on another wall. Darren's house had an open floor plan with a living room, a dining area and a kitchen with stainless steel appliances. Pretty but plain in neutral shades. The opposite wall was floor-to-ceiling windows.

Stepping closer to the windows, she peered outside. Woods surrounded most of Darren's property, but there was an open field to the left that went on for days. Rolling hills beyond completed the idyllic view.

"I'll be right back." Darren disappeared down a short hallway into what must have been his bedroom.

Bree barely heard him. She walked around, touching the stone fireplace and scoping out the upstairs loft with a wrought iron railing facing those windows. What a perfect spot to practice her cello with such an inspiring view. Too bad the music room at Bay Willows faced the little post office instead of the lake.

"Here, that should do it, and your feet will stay warm."

She took the thick woolen socks from him. "Thank you. You have a beautiful view."

He narrowed his gaze as if questioning her sincerity. "I think so."

Maybe his ex-fiancée hadn't thought so. Maybe the plain walls other than dead animals didn't appeal. The waders Bree had tried on had to have been Raleigh's. They were too small for Darren. Somehow Bree couldn't picture Stella's tall, model-like granddaughter trussed up in rubber waders. Bree couldn't imagine her here, either, amid the multiple shades of tan and lack of artwork. The lack of flair.

He gave her an odd look as if considering her for something. "Follow me."

Bree's stomach flipped. "Where?"

But he was already in the kitchen, opening the fridge and pulling out a pot.

"What's that?"

He lifted the lid and plunged a fork inside. "Venison stew. Wanna try it?"

Bree wrinkled her nose. "Cold?"

He chuckled. "Not quite. I had it for dinner tonight."

She hesitated, not sure she wanted to venture quite that far, but then squared her shoulders. This outing was about trying new things. She stepped forward, waders and socks in hand.

Darren held the fork for her, cupping his hand underneath. "Go ahead."

She stalled, looking into his eyes. "You made this?"

He laughed. A low, soft rumble that sounded incredibly masculine. "Don't worry. I can cook."

Bree took in the forkful offered and chewed. The venison was still warm and surprisingly tasty. She glanced at Darren again.

He watched her closely. "Well?"

"Good." Her voice came out sounding strangely hoarse.

It was then that Bree saw her attraction reflected back from Darren's blue eyes. He had to feel it, too—this strange stirring of the senses. For a moment, the only thing she heard was the increased beat of her pulse pounding like crazy.

He stepped back and set the fork in the sink with a clatter. "Ready?"

Bree nodded. "As ready as I'll ever be, I suppose."

Darren chuckled as he returned the pot to the fridge. "Let's go."

She blew out her breath and followed him back downstairs. Slipping into her sneakers and then clutching the heavy woolen socks and waders close, she climbed into Darren's white pickup truck. What had just happened?

"I can put those in the back," Darren offered as he clicked on the radio and country music whispered.

"I'm good." Bree spied the slim backseat and clutched the socks and waders closer as if they'd protect her from the odd sensations flooding her.

Darren turned up the volume to an upbeat song that crooned about the mysteries between a man and a woman. Hearing some guy sing about kissing in the morning didn't help. Not at all. Bree tapped her toe on the floor in time with the beat, hoping to dispel whatever it was that Darren had done to her with merely a smile.

She'd never met anyone like Darren before. Having grown up downstate, Bree hadn't been exposed to things like venison, guns or smelt dipping. Was she ready for what lay ahead?

A shiver raced through her despite the warmth of the truck's heater. Tonight promised something she craved. Not only a break from her usual routine but also adventurous freedom before she made one of the biggest time commitments of her life.

She'd wanted a change, and tonight definitely ranked as different. Only, she hoped this inconvenient attraction to Darren would pass. She'd worked with nice-looking musicians without any trouble. Maybe this was merely a temporary curiosity because Darren wasn't like the urbane men she was used to. He was different. A passing fancy that would eventually vanish. Once her vacation was over.

Darren parked his truck next to his friend's SUV and got out. The pungently sweet smell of burning wood hung in the air. There were several other vehicles parked in the small clearing off a two-track path. The place was crowded.

He looked up at the clear sky tinted pink with the memory of this evening's sunset. A big crescent moon hung just above the tree line. It wouldn't shed much light later—not quite the blue moonlight he'd promised—but then, he had flashlights.

"Something wrong?" Bree climbed out of his truck.

"Our moon is nothing but a weak sliver tonight."

She looked up. "Still very pretty."

Like her.

He slipped into his waders. "You'd better put yours on. The grass looks wet." He handed her a pair of the smallest work gloves he had. "Here. Those thin knit gloves you're wearing won't keep you warm. You can slip these on top as protection against the cold when dipping nets."

"Thanks." Bree settled back in the passenger seat and slipped off her sneakers. She made quick work of getting into the wool socks and waders that were too long for her. She stuffed her cell phone and the gloves he gave her into the front pocket, shut the truck's door and joined him. "Ready."

Darren nodded, scanning her from head to toe. "Are you warm enough? I have an extra sweatshirt in the truck."

"I'm good." She wore a dark brown knit hat that matched her hair. Hair that had been gathered into a long, fat braid.

"Here, follow me." He handed her a stack of buckets while he carried their nets and a couple of flashlights, and they made their way toward the river.

Lantern lights and bonfires shone from various spots along the wooded shoreline. Dark water with glimmers of reflected light gurgled as it flowed. He heard raucous laughter but nothing worse. He might be off duty, but if anyone got out of hand, he'd take a look. They weren't the only ones out here hoping to enjoy the evening. He'd do what he could to make sure it stayed enjoyable—for everyone.

"Hey." His friend Neil gave them a wave.

Kate, Neil's wife, openly gaped, surprised to see him with a woman. Especially a woman like Bree. "'Bout time."

Darren ignored the double meaning. Kate had been after him to date someone, anyone, as long as he quit dwelling on his ex. He quickly made the introductions. "Any smelt?"

"We've caught a few." Neil tipped his bucket to reveal a small pile of little silver fish.

He glanced at Bree, standing by the fire with her bare hands stretched toward the heat. The waders he'd purchased as a gift for Raleigh were too big for her. They bunched around Bree's knees and ankles, making her look like a girl playing dress-up in adult clothes. "Ready to give it a try?"

She walked toward him, nearly tripping. "That's what I'm here for."

He should have noticed how long the waders were before they'd left the house. But then, her presence had knocked him a bit off kilter. Darren fished around in the front pocket of his waders and found what he'd wanted.

He held up a decent length of thin rope. "Come here."

She looked at it, eyes wide and wary. "What for?"

He pulled the rope taut and laughed. "I'm not going to tie you up. It's a belt. Pull those waders up as high as you can."

"Oh." The relief in her voice made him smile as she stepped forward. "You know, it's not very nice to brandish a rope like that."

"I'll remember that." He looped the rope around her

waist and brought her close. Much too close. He inhaled
that soft, flowery scent she wore and tied the rope with
an awkward jerk that nearly landed her against his chest.
He glanced at her face. Those plump lips of hers tempted,
but what knocked him for a loop were her golden eyes
wide with wonder.

She studied him.

He focused on her shoulder straps. "Better?"

"Much better. Thank you." Her voice sounded breathless.

Darren quickly stepped back before he did something
stupid. He looked around to get his bearings and spotted
Neil and Kate with their nets ready. They watched him
and Bree instead of heading into the river.

Neil gave him a *thattaboy* nod.

Darren shook his head. Even though he found Bree attractive, he wasn't going to act on his feelings. No way.
"Ready to wade in?"

"I am."

"Okay, watch your step. The rocks are slippery. We
don't have to go very far. The smelt pool close to shore."
He flashed the light. "See, there are a few right there."

Bree gripped his arm tightly and leaned over for a peek.
"Look at that."

"You can stay on shore and dip if you want."

She shook her head. "Nope, I'm going in, but can I hold
on to you?"

Those simple words pierced, reminding him that Raleigh hadn't wanted to hold on. She'd cut him loose to swim
in a faster stream. He couldn't let Bree get under his skin.
She was leaving; Maple Springs wasn't enough to keep her
happy. He wouldn't be enough to keep her happy either.

"Yeah, sure." Darren put some distance between them

to arrange their buckets along the shoreline. He handed her a net and then offered his hand.

She slipped on the gloves he'd given her. They were too big. He held tight while her eyes darted nervously along the river's edge. "You won't let go?"

"Not till you say it's okay."

She slowly followed him into the river.

The dark water was high from the winter snow melt and the current a little stronger than normal, but certainly not fast and not deep. Not where they stood up to their knees. Something about the way Bree trusted him to keep her safe made him want to do just that. "I'm going to pull you to me so you can dip your net in, okay?"

She nodded.

He wrapped his arm around her trim waist and shone the flashlight on the water, giving up flashes of silver from beneath the surface. "Go ahead and dip your net in. I got you."

Bree dipped her net with one hand while holding on to his waders with the other. She wasn't taking any chances. She pulled up a few smelt and laughed at the squirming little fish.

"It's as easy as that," he said.

She looked up at him smiling. Her golden eyes looked darker at night, and the creases of her dimples faded with her smile. "Now what?"

His gaze strayed to her mouth. He wouldn't mind smearing that lipstick. "We put them in the buckets."

She let go of him. "I think I can do this."

He loosened his hold. "I know you can."

It wasn't that hard to stay upright, but then, Bree had never done this before. He watched her make her way back to shore, where she emptied her net. Then she carefully trudged back to him, refusing his offer of a steady hand.

Neil and Kate were in the water ahead of them.

"So, what do you do with all of these smelt?"

"We clean and then fry them."

"Are they good?" She looked doubtful.

"You'll have to find out for yourself." A fish fry meant another outing with Bree, unless she declined. But seeing the rapt expression on her face, he realized that wasn't going to happen. She clearly enjoyed this.

"But they're so small."

"You liked the venison, right?"

"Right." Bree dipped her net again, bringing in a few more. "Hey, look at that load."

They dipped and dumped until they'd nearly filled a gallon bucket. Bree's teeth chattered, but she hadn't complained. Not once.

"Ready for a break? We can warm up by the fire."

"Yess-ss."

He held out his hand to help her back to shore. She took it, letting go as soon as they were safe and sound on the river's bank. Kate and Neil were already seated around the fire, roasting hot dogs on sticks.

"Want one?" Kate offered him the package. "Bree, there's also pop and water in the cooler."

"Thank you." Bree stood close to the fire. Her phone buzzed, and she pulled it out from deep within the waders. Her mouth formed a grim line when she looked at it.

"Everything okay?" He grabbed a stick, skewered a dog onto it and then offered it to Bree before fixing a double for himself.

"It's nothing." She slipped her phone back where it came from and held her stick over the flames. "How often do you guys do this?"

"Once a year. Maybe twice, but it's a short spawning run. There are not nearly as many smelt as when my dad brought me here years ago," Kate said. "And with the DNR's limit of only two gallons per person…"

Darren laughed. "I don't write the rules. I enforce them."

"But not tonight." Neil poked his stick downriver at the other smelt dippers.

Darren shrugged. "Not unless I see something troubling."

Bree's eyes widened, but she didn't say anything.

He didn't look for trouble, but if he saw it, he'd do something about it. It was what he did. It was who he was.

Bree turned to Kate. "So, you grew up here?"

"I did, yes. What about you? Just here for the summer?" How'd Kate guess that? But then, one look at Bree confirmed she wasn't a local. If the red lipstick wasn't a dead giveaway, it was everything else about her. The way she moved, dressed, even talked with that slight lilt in her voice.

"My family owns a summer cottage in Bay Willows. I'm staying for a few weeks before moving out west." Bree rolled her hot dog and watched it sizzle.

Kate flashed him a look of concern.

Yeah, okay, maybe he was a glutton for punishment.

"How'd you two meet?" Kate asked.

"My mom organized a wild edibles class and Darren is our facilitator." Bree reached for a bun.

"Oh, nice." Kate handed over the mustard.

With his hot dogs roasted to perfection and nestled inside buns, Darren offered Bree a seat on an overturned bucket by the fire. It didn't take him long to wolf down his first dog. He glanced at Bree. She squeezed a dainty line of mustard along the center of her hot dog and ate with precise, ladylike bites.

"Back in the pond, I see." Neil stood next to him.

Darren splattered mustard on his second hot dog and took a bite. "Not even testing the waters."

"Right." Neil laughed at him.

Before Darren could protest, he spotted a beam of light that bobbed along the path they'd come down. A fellow conservation officer stepped through the brush, checking smelt limits. Stan nodded toward him. "Hey, Darren. How'd you guys do?"

"Just a couple of buckets. Not much, but enough."

"No trouble this evening?"

"Tame crowd," Darren answered.

"Good. I'm hoping for an early night." Stan hesitated. "When will you hear about Teri's spot?"

"I don't know. Soon." Darren finished his second hot dog.

"We're pulling for you."

"Thanks," Darren said.

Stan gave them a wave. "Good night."

"So, you're going for the area supervisor position again?" Neil asked.

Darren nodded. "Yep."

"It'll steep you pretty deep in town. You sure you want that?"

Like he needed a warning. "I know."

"Wait, what's wrong with in town?" Bree asked.

"The summer crowd drives him nuts."

"Oh? And why's that?" Bree cocked her head in challenge. She looked about as tough as an angry kitten.

Darren shrugged. "I don't like crowds."

"Not to mention he hasn't set foot in downtown Maple Springs in over a year and a half." Neil gave him a teasing shove. "That right?"

"Pretty much sums it up." Darren stretched. He wasn't

getting into any of his reasons why. Not here, not with Bree. "I'm going to dip some more."

Bree stood. "I'll go, too. I want to get that limit."

"You going to clean them?" Amazed that she was into this, Darren had thrown down the challenge.

She picked it right up. "If you show me how."

"Tomorrow night, my house. We'll clean and fix what we catch here." He gestured toward Kate and Neil. "I'll invite them, too."

"Deal." Bree waded in next to him without any assistance.

She dipped like a pro. Not that it was hard, but he hadn't expected her to take to it so quickly. Raleigh would never have done this. She wouldn't have tried venison, either. Bree had nerve. He'd give her that.

The night wore on, and when they finally packed up to head for home, Darren noticed Bree huddled in the passenger seat, looking frozen. "It'll take a minute or two before the heat kicks in."

Bree considered him. "Is it true that you haven't been in town for almost two years?"

"I go to church, and that's downtown." Instead of expanding, Darren joked, "It's better not to listen to what Neil says."

Bree kept digging. "Is it because of Stella's granddaughter?"

"Something like that." He didn't want to come face-to-face with her and Tony and react. He didn't want to talk about it, either.

"Oh." Bree's brow furrowed, but she got the message and let it drop.

He drove the rest of the way home in silence. It wasn't far, but Bree had put her head back and closed her eyes.

Surely she hadn't fallen asleep that fast, but then, it was after one in the morning when he turned into his driveway.

Bree sat up straight and looked around, getting her bearings. She *had* fallen asleep.

Nice. He put women to sleep. That was about right. Boring local yokel. Nothing exciting here. He cleared his throat. "Be careful driving back to town."

She looked confused at his sharp tone. "Don't you want help unloading the smelt?"

"No. I got it." He was confused by his sudden irritation, too. He suddenly didn't like the idea of her driving alone in the wee hours, but unless he followed her home, there wasn't much else he could do. He couldn't offer that she stay here. "Keep an eye out for deer and drive slow."

She narrowed her gaze, looking offended, as if he'd told her she couldn't take care of herself. "Would you like me to text you when I get home?"

Her sarcasm wasn't lost on him. "Yeah, do that. I'm serious. Deer move at night."

"Okay, okay. See you tomorrow." She slid behind the wheel of her small Subaru and rolled down the window as if she'd forgotten something. "Thanks, Darren, for taking me smelt dipping."

Surprised at her sincerity, he gave her a nod. "You're welcome."

He unloaded the truck as she backed out. Placing the smelt in the extra refrigerator he had in the garage, he couldn't believe he looked forward to tomorrow night. Would Bree surprise him yet again by cleaning their catch?

Twenty minutes later, he got his answer when his phone whistled with Bree's incoming text.

Made it home fine. Thanks again for tonight. I had a great time off the beaten path.

He smiled and texted back, It was fun. He meant it.

Really fun! Looking forward to cleaning 2morrow. Good night.

Good night.

He slipped his phone in his pocket.

Bree might be cut from the same cloth as Raleigh, but her pattern was completely different. Bree had treated Kate and Neil with warm respect, and they'd jumped on the fish fry invitation. They liked her.

He did, too.

Maybe all Bree wanted was to have fun, plain and simple. Nothing complicated. There was no reason they couldn't keep things that way. Maybe if he showed Bree a good time, he'd learn to have fun again, too. He needed that more than he cared to admit. It didn't mean anything had to change. He wouldn't have to change.

He could be friends with a woman without having to date her. Without needing to kiss her. Even Bree. Most especially Bree.

Chapter Five

"I'm heading out." Bree slipped on a cotton cardigan sweater over her T-shirt.

The warm day had dissolved into a chilly evening. Tonight she'd head to Darren's for their smelt dinner, and she'd pick up something at the store on her way to take. Maybe he'd build a fire in that huge fireplace of his and they could hang out and watch the flames dance.

Or maybe not. Really, where'd that idea come from?

"Philip called while you were out walking," her mother said.

Bree's good mood took a nosedive. She'd had her cell phone with her the whole time. Odd. Why didn't he call or text her? "What did he want?"

"He wanted to make sure you were okay."

Bree narrowed her gaze. "I'm fine."

"Maybe he's reconsidering."

"Reconsidering what?" *Being an idiot?* Bree didn't voice that thought.

"Breaking up. We had a long chat, and he's concerned for you."

"Concerned?" Bree should have set the record straight, but what was the point? If Philip wanted to think he'd ended it, fine. As long as he truly ended it and left her alone.

"What if you regret this decision? Seattle is a big move, and two years is a long time."

Bree gritted her teeth. She didn't need Philip stirring up more doubt in her parents' heads. The music residency couldn't have come at a better time. If she didn't spread her wings a little, she'd never know if she could fly. "This is the opportunity of a lifetime."

Her mother didn't look convinced. "But men like Philip don't grow on trees."

At twenty-nine, Bree was old enough to make her own decisions, but her parents still wanted her tucked into a prestigious marriage like the one her sister had. She grabbed her purse. "He's not for me."

"Surely you're not enamored with this DNR fella you're going to see."

"No, Mom, I'm not." She'd explained that Darren's friends would be there, too. This wasn't a date or any-thing. Besides, *attracted* wasn't even close to *enamored*. She'd be safe. "For the next twenty-four months, I won't have time for any *fella*."

Bree meant that, even though her heart skipped at the thought of Darren near that fireplace. "I've got to go."

"Oh, one more thing. Jan Nelson called. She wondered if you'd play next weekend for the Mother's Day brunch at the Maple Springs Inn. They need a cello."

"Sure, I'll call her." Jan was a board member of the Bay Willows Association and the driving force behind starting a summer music school. It was probably going to be some kind of music camp for kids, but Bree wouldn't mind finding out if there were future plans for anything more intensive.

"And Philip?"

Bree let out a sigh. "I'll let him know I'm fine."

Her mother smiled. "Thank you and be careful."

"I will." Careful might as well have been her middle name.

As a teen, Bree had never roughhoused or played sports like her sister for fear of any injury keeping her away from the cello. As a college student, she'd buried herself with a double major in performing arts and music composition. Then there'd been overseas opportunities and getting her master's while making her way up within the strings section of the symphony orchestra. Where was the fun, frivolous stuff?

Tonight she'd clean fish with Darren and his friends. *She'd clean fish!* That's something she'd never done before. She might not like it once she saw what it entailed, but Bree wanted no regrets and no missed opportunities. She needed to do fun stuff before focusing every ounce of her energy on music once again.

Could she compete at the level she was about to step up to? She had to. Bree wanted more than playing someone else's music all the time. She'd create her own, have it heard and somehow make an impact.

With God's grace, she'd figure it all out. But she had to be proactive. That meant cleaning the small silvery fish she'd helped catch the night before while standing in a freezing-cold river with a burly man she barely knew. That kind of gumption was what she needed to practice more of if she wanted to succeed.

"So, what's with you and Bree?" Kate cornered Darren in the kitchen.

He shrugged. "She wants to experience new things, and I offered to show her the area."

Kate looked skeptical. "Uh-huh."

"Hey, you're the one who said I should start dating."

That made his friend's wife look even more concerned. "I meant someone local, not someone who's moving away in a month. A lot can happen in a month."

He knew all about that. "Nothing will happen at all. We're just having some fun."

"Leave him alone, Kate." Neil carried in a bucket of the smelt and set it on the table, followed by Darren's brother Cam.

"Who's Bree?" Cam asked.

Darren clenched his teeth before he snarled at all of them. "No one. Look, it's no big deal. She's not looking to get involved and neither am I. Besides, she's not my type."

"She's exactly your type," Neil said with a laugh.

Darren looked at him sharply. "What's that supposed to mean?"

"She's different, and you like different."

Cam laughed. "He's got a point."

That much was probably true. Darren had dated his share, not finding anyone he'd wanted to settle down with until Raleigh had knocked him for a loop. His ex-fiancée had been nothing like the girls he'd gone out with before. Nothing like his sisters either, who'd grown up knowing how to take care of themselves out-of-doors.

"No one from Bay Willows is my type," Darren grumbled. He'd been there, done that. And he wouldn't do it again. Not if he was smart.

A knock at the door scattered his thoughts. Glancing toward the storm door, he saw Bree standing on the other side, and his pulse picked up speed. Was she truly different? Probably not. She might look different, but where she came from made her the same as everything he didn't want.

He opened the door. "Hey."

Bree looked around. "Where are your dogs?"

"Downstairs until after we eat."

She lifted a brown paper bag. "I brought a few things for dinner."

"Great." He peeked inside at a container of coleslaw next to chocolate bars, marshmallows and graham crackers. "S'mores?"

"I thought maybe later by the fire—" She looked a little flustered. "They make good dessert."

"Yeah, sure." He backed away to let her pass. Her hair had been twisted into a knot at the back of her head, and she wore a soft yellow sweater and jeans. She looked great. Much too nice to scoop the guts out of smelt.

"You sure you want to do this?"

She stopped walking and looked up at him, wrinkling her nose. "Is it really bad?"

He chuckled. "No. It's just…"

Her gaze narrowed. "What?"

He glanced at her shoulders. "That looks like a good sweater."

"No worries. I've got a T-shirt underneath." She turned and headed for the kitchen.

Darren scratched his head and followed her. She might change her tune once they got the assembly line set up. But then, something about the determined line of those narrow shoulders told him she was on a mission.

He wasn't sure what that was all about, but hearing her give Kate and Neil a warm greeting did something to him. Something scary. He got the crazy impression that his house felt more like a home with her in it.

"And this is my brother Cam. He's staying for dinner, too." Darren was glad for that. It made the night less like a double date.

Bree held out her hand. "Nice to meet you."

"Likewise." Cam gave her a wink.

Bree quickly pulled away and headed for the fireplace. Her eyes glowed. "You built a fire!"

"To take the chill off." Darren didn't know what else to say. She looked so pleased, and he wished his friends and brother were anywhere else but here.

"See, those s'mores will come in handy." Her dimples showed.

He'd never roasted marshmallows inside before, but doing that with Bree seemed dangerous somehow. "Huh."

She slipped off her sweater, revealing a white top that was far from his idea of a simple T-shirt with its ruffled hem. "So, what do we do now?"

Neil gave Cam a pointed look. "Maybe we should disappear."

Cam laughed and headed for the recliner. "I'm watching the news."

Darren quit gawking. He was thinking too much about making those s'mores. "We'll set up an assembly line to clean, dredge and then fry up the smelt."

Bree padded straight to his sink and washed her hands. "I'm ready."

Kate laughed. "You might want to work at my end with the flour and frying."

Bree shook her head. "No way. I caught them. I need to learn how to clean them."

Kate raised her eyebrows and glanced at him.

Darren shrugged. One thing he'd learned about Bree— she went at a task with determination. He'd never seen anyone work this hard to *have fun*. "Let me show you what to do, and then you can decide."

He grabbed the half-full bucket of smelt and set it next to the sink, then washed up. Taking one of the small fish in one hand and scissors in the other, he turned to Bree. "First, we make a cut at the back of the head, and then another cut along the underside starting from the tail, like so, up toward the head."

Bree watched closely. "Then what?"

"Then gently pull the head away and all the innards come with it. See?" He showed her the cleaned out smelt. It wasn't a messy process. Cleaning smelt was easier than filleting other fish. It simply took longer because there were more of them. "We rinse them real good, bread them and fry them."

"Okay." She sounded a little shaky.

He laughed. "You don't have to do this."

Bree stared at the smelt. "Yes, I do."

"Why? What's with all this trying new things?"

She squared her shoulders. "It's a confidence booster."

This woman seemed confident to him. Her choppy bangs screamed that she didn't care what people thought, but maybe it was all a ruse. A front to hide behind, like Raleigh had hidden behind that rebellious spirit of hers.

He wanted to know why Bree needed a confidence boost, but he didn't ask. The less he knew about her down deep, the better. "Want to cut or clean?"

Looking like she approached a dissection assignment in science class, Bree considered the options, then finally answered, "I don't think I can use scissors like that, so I'll do the cleaning."

"Alright, let's get started." He glanced at Neil, who'd finished making the flour coating. "We'll get a few cleaned in advance."

His buddy grabbed a couple of beverages from the fridge and joined his wife and Cam in the living room to catch the local news. "Take your time."

Darren looked at Bree. "Ready?"

"Yes."

He made the cut and handed the fish over.

She tried to grab the head, hesitated and then tried again.

"Like this." Darren covered her hand with his own. "Stick your index finger in where I made the cut here and then pull down."

She looked up at him, her eyes wide and inviting.

Darren didn't look away. "See, not bad."

"No. Not bad at all." Her voice sounded soft and a little breathless.

Awareness kicked him hard. He wasn't so sure they were talking about the fish. He quickly let go of her hand, concentrated on the next smelt and handed it over. "Here, try on your own."

Bree did as asked, without hesitation this time. Then she rinsed the fish off and tossed it in the big stainless steel bowl he'd placed on the counter next to her.

"Good job."

"Thanks." She reached for the next one.

Darren obliged with one smelt after the other. Soon Bree was cleaning them like a pro, but she refused to cut the heads. They kicked up the pace when Kate joined them to heat up the oil in a big fry pan.

They'd soon have dinner, and then what? Roasting marshmallows by the fire sure sounded like something to do on a date. He hoped Neil and Kate didn't leave early. Cam would no doubt duck out after dinner.

All Darren knew was that he didn't want to be left alone with Bree.

Bree took a deep breath when dinner was finally on the table. She needed to sit as far away from Darren as possible. It was bad enough standing close by the sink where their fingers touched every time he handed her a smelt.

Maybe she'd imagined the mushroom cloud of awareness that had billowed between them. Maybe it was all one-sided. Hers. Explosive attraction was foreign to her. She'd never felt this way with Philip. Was never drawn to him the way Darren pulled at her with invisible strings.

"Let's pray so we can eat." Kate sat down and reached for her husband's hand on one side and Cam's on the other.

Oh, no. Not more hand-holding. Bree slipped into the only open chair across from Kate, putting her right next Darren. Okay, maybe sitting next to him, she wouldn't get lost in his bright blue eyes.

"Neil, do you mind?" He wrapped his hand around hers. Darren had honest hands, calloused in spots and work-worn. Warm and strong.

Bree bowed her head and listened to the prayer of gratitude for the food. Surprised when Neil mentioned her name, she looked up.

"Guide her, Lord, in this next step of her life. Amen."

Darren surprised her even more by squeezing her hand before letting go. No one had ever prayed so specifically for her before. She looked at Neil. "Thank you."

Neil smiled. "You're welcome."

"So, what's up?" Cam asked.

"I'm moving to Seattle for a music residency there." Bree accepted the platter of fried smelt and stared at it. She'd caught them, cleaned them, and now it was time to eat them. Could she do it?

"Don't worry about the bones," Cam said. "You can't tell they're even there."

Bree nodded and scooped a few onto her plate.

"How long will you be gone?" Cam asked.

"Two years." Bree looked around the table, watching the others fill their plates. She took a tentative bite of fish.

It was good. Really good. So when the platter was set before her, she grabbed a few more.

"Will you stay out there afterward, then? At the end you'll have a job waiting for you?" Kate offered her the bowl of coleslaw.

"Maybe." A lot depended on her. Was she good enough actually to compose? She wouldn't ever give up her cello, but it'd be nice to do more, maybe even mentor others. There were tons of opportunities out west where the music business spanned so much wider for composition than here, in the Midwest.

"We may never see you again," Kate said.

Bree knew this had been stated for Darren's benefit. His friends were trying to protect him. From her. It was laughable considering how timid she'd been dating Philip. Until recently, she'd never rocked the boat. It wouldn't be smart to get involved with someone whose roots were planted so deep here. "I suppose that might be true."

"Her parents have a place in Bay Willows." Darren winked at her.

Bree smiled. "I guess I'll be back sometime. I can't imagine a better place for summer vacations."

"I can. It's called the Bahamas," Neil said.

They all laughed.

Bree turned to Darren. "Where do you go on vacation?"

Darren shrugged. "The Upper Peninsula, mostly. My uncle has a camp there."

Bree tipped her head. "Like a whole campground?"

He chuckled. "No, it's a cabin on a small lake."

"I've never been to the UP."

He looked at her, shocked. "Never been over the bridge?"

She shrugged. There had never been a reason to go. "Nope."

"Something you should remedy before you leave." Cam scooped more smelt onto his plate.

"Oh, I've seen it. I've been to Mackinac Island." Bree knew the beauty of the five-mile-long Mighty Mac. She'd even toured the bridge museum in Mackinaw City.

"Take her for a burger at that drive-in restaurant," Neil said.

Darren chuckled. "Yeah, maybe."

Bree didn't jump on that one. It sounded too much like a real date, and she wasn't looking to *date* Darren. Getting to know him better was fine, as long as it remained friendly. "I think I'd rather see those elk roaming."

Darren nodded. "We can do that."

Cam looked aghast, as if they were both crazy. "Yeah, there's a real good time."

Bree glanced between brothers. The resemblance was strong, but Cam was blond and struck her as a flirt.

Finished with dinner, Bree helped Kate clear the table while the guys took the makings for s'mores into the living room.

Bree handed Kate the platter with a few leftover smelt.

"Thanks." Kate hesitated as if grappling with something she wanted to say.

"What?" Bree prodded.

Kate waved her hand in dismissal. "Nothing."

Bree knew it was something and more than likely something about Darren. And her. "I know you're concerned for him because of his broken engagement and all."

Kate's eyes grew wide. "He told you about that?"

"Stella, Raleigh's grandmother, is a friend of mine. She told me her granddaughter broke it off."

"Did she tell you how?" Kate glanced into the living room to be sure they weren't overheard. The guys had the

TV tuned into a baseball game. The volume was up and they were loud too.

Bree had never been very good at listening or remembering rumors, but the look on Kate's face clued her in that this wasn't going to be good. "No. Not really."

"He won't talk about it." Kate lowered her voice to a mere whisper. "But his bride ran off with the best man the night before the wedding."

Bree's stomach dropped. "Wow…"

"Yeah. 'Wow.' He's had a rough time of it." Kate loaded up the dishwasher with the plates Bree had stacked on the counter.

"It's no wonder." And no wonder he was wary. Bree couldn't imagine the sting of that kind of betrayal.

Kate stopped arranging dishes and looked at Bree. "He fell pretty hard and got engaged only a month after meeting her."

Bree's mind whirled. She gripped the counter as if it were the room spinning and not her thoughts. Her heart. Darren didn't dawdle when it came to falling in love.

"You two coming in or what?" Darren poked his head around the corner.

Bree glanced at Kate. Had he heard them?

"We're on our way." Kate gave her a pointed look, then whispered, "He'd have a fit if he knew I'd told you."

Bree made a zipping gesture across her lips. Walking into the living room, Bree drew close to the hearth and sat down on the floor. The snap and crackle of the fire soothed, but she couldn't get what Kate said out of her head. Only a month. He'd decided to spend the rest of his life with someone after only a month.

Would Darren truly be mad if he knew that she knew?

"Here." Darren handed her one of a handful of metal skewers with a couple marshmallows stuck on the end.

"Thanks." She held it over the flames, watching the white puff of sugar slowly turn brown. The mellow warmth of burning wood coupled with a hearty dinner made Bree's eyelids droop.

"Tired?" Darren sat next to her.

Maybe she was too comfortable here, hanging out with Darren's friends and even his brother. And maybe she wanted to know more than she should about this man who once gave his heart so easily. She raised her s'more. "After this, I'd better go."

"Thanks for coming."

"Are you kidding? It was great. I like smelt. The whole thing."

Darren laughed. "You did good cleaning them."

The compliment warmed her more than the fire. "Thanks."

"Here, your marshmallow's about to fall." Darren held out a graham cracker layered with chocolate.

Bree concentrated on getting the wobbly mass of mallow in between the crackers without dropping it and then laughed when she succeeded. "Aren't you having one?"

Darren shrugged. "Not much of a s'more guy."

"I love these things. In a pinch, I've made them over the gas stove in my apartment." Bree took a bite, smearing melted chocolate all over the corner of her mouth. A gooey bit of marshmallow stuck to her chin. She wiped it off with the heel of her hand. Her fingers were sticky, too.

"You have chocolate right here, in that crazy dimple." Darren wiped near her cheek.

Bree froze, hardly breathing.

"I do like chocolate." He licked his thumb. "And dimples."

She panicked at the softness of Darren's voice and glanced toward the couch. Kate and Neil snuggled at one end, glued to the ball game, and Darren's brother had gone into the kitchen and returned with a glass of water. She connected with his smirking gaze, and her stomach turned. Had he seen them?

Cam gave her a saucy wink.

She felt her cheeks flush with heat. That answered that. She needed to get out of here fast. Another two bites and her s'more was gone. Bree brushed her hands off on her jeans and stood. "I'm going to head home."

Darren stood, too. "I'll walk you to the door."

"Thanks."

"Good night, Bree." Kate gave her a wave, and her husband did the same.

"Be careful," Cam said and then chuckled.

Bree knew her face was on fire. The rest of her was, too. Really, this wasn't good. She heard the beagles bellow from downstairs and was grateful for the distraction. "Your dogs?"

"They want up."

"Aww, I didn't get to see them." Bree wasn't about to stay, though.

"Next time." Darren opened the door and leaned against the frame. "You okay to drive home?"

"I'll be fine." But she'd stifled a yawn. "I'll text you when I get there."

The dogs barked again.

Bree needed to leave. She opened the storm door, glad for the cool night air. "See you at class."

"Good night, Bree." His deep voice sounded dangerously sweet.

"Night." She scrambled off the deck and skipped down the steps as quickly as possible.

She'd had fun this evening. Maybe too much fun, and certainly too much food and too much of Darren. Near him, she got a heady feeling as if she'd drunk wine. Not good.

Slipping into the driver's seat, she started her car, and her phone buzzed from inside her purse. She'd left it in the car. Two messages from Philip. One a text, the other a voice mail with an agitated male voice asking where she was.

Pulling out of the driveway, she returned the call.

"Bree, 'bout time—"

She cut him off. "Philip, this has got to stop. Why do you keep calling me?"

"I want to make sure you're okay."

"I'm fine."

"Still accepting that residency?"

"I'm not backing out." Not for anything.

Silence.

"Philip, I've got to go. I'm driving. And please stop calling."

"Driving? Where are you?"

"That's none of your concern." Her voice sounded shrill.

"Fine." He sounded annoyed. Then his tone softened. "Okay. Take care, Bree."

Maybe this would be it. Maybe he'd finally gotten the message that they were through. "You, too."

The chill air made her shiver. Rolling up her window, she reached for her sweater and realized she'd left it at Darren's. She'd text him to bring it to class when she got home.

Home.

Here couldn't be home. There were no opportunities for her here. Right now, she didn't have a place to call home, and yet there was something about the way Darren made her feel at home with him. She thought about what Kate had told her. Darren had asked Raleigh to marry him after only a month. She'd never thought that possible before. Never thought feelings could be real after such a short time. But now—

She repeated what she'd told Philip out loud and with volume. "I'm not backing out of this residency. Not for anything or anyone."

Chapter Six

Sunday morning, Darren stepped out of the church he'd attended all his life. He still went where his parents went along with some of his siblings. He didn't see any reason to change. Attending his traditional church service was the one place he didn't worry about running into Tony or Raleigh.

His reluctance to try another church had been one of the many bones of contention he'd had with his ex-fiancée. He liked going where he'd gone since childhood, but Raleigh didn't. In hindsight, maybe he should have been more flexible, tried someplace else. It was too easy to go through the motions here, where he'd never had to get involved deeper than simply showing up.

"Brrr…" His mom pulled her jacket closer. "It's chilly today."

"Supposed to get even colder." His dad stood on the wide church steps and surveyed downtown.

"Not expected to warm up for a few days yet." Usually in a rush to leave, today Darren wasn't in a hurry to head for his empty home. He followed his father's gaze over Maple Springs. The leaves on the trees were still young with that spring-green crayon color. Main Street lay sleepy on this cold morning before the town swelled with summer residents and tourists.

"As long as it doesn't snow on Mother's Day, I'm good." His mom tucked her arm into the crook of Darren's elbow. "Come to breakfast with us. It's your favorite place."

Simply called Dean's Hometown Grille, the tiny restaurant was right around the corner and probably packed. He used to go there a lot with Tony. Darren swallowed hard. Maybe he wasn't feeling *that* brave.

"Hey, isn't that your girlfriend over there?" Cam had exited the church and pointed.

Darren spotted Bree walking toward them from across the street. "She's not my girlfriend."

His mom's eyes widened. "Why didn't you tell me you're seeing someone?"

"Darren's got a girlfriend? Will wonders never cease?" His sister Monica joined the gawkers. "Who is she?"

"Just a friend." There was no use correcting them. They wouldn't believe him, anyway.

Bree waved and crossed the street. Pretty in dark leggings and a long sweater, she headed straight for them with a smile that made those dimples flash. She wore the same brown knitted hat, and her hair was gathered into one long, fat braid.

His pulse kicked up a notch. *Great. Just great.*

When Bree stood at the base of the church steps, she smiled again. "Morning Darren, Cam."

"Meet my family. Some of them, anyway." Darren should have left when he'd had the chance.

"So, this is where you go to church. I go to the Bay Willows chapel." Before he could stop the inevitable, Bree extended a hand toward his mom. "Hi, I'm Bree Anderson."

"Helen Zelinsky." His mom eagerly returned the handshake. "And this is my husband, Andy. My daughter Monica, and you've met Cam."

"Last night at Darren's," Cam added.

His mom gave him that questioning look Darren knew to answer. "Bree is helping out with the wild edibles class at Bay Willows."

"Oh." His mom's eyes widened a bit more before focusing back on Bree. "How's he doing?"

"Wonderful. He really knows his stuff." Bree gave him a nod. "I saw Stella at services this morning, and we're looking forward to hunting for fiddleheads."

Darren nodded. "They can be elusive, but they're out there."

They fell into an awkward silence.

"Well, I'd better get back home." Bree dipped her head.

"We're headed for breakfast around the corner. Please, join us." His mom used her *don't-refuse-me* tone.

Darren could have kicked his mom, but letting Bree walk away would open up a can of questions he didn't feel like answering. He'd feel safer if she joined them. "You won't be sorry. The food's plain but good."

"Yeah?" Bree looked as if she weighed his words.

He meant it, and threw out a ready excuse. "Buying your breakfast is the least I can do considering your help with the class."

"Showing me the area is more than enough thanks."

His mom jumped on that like his beagles swarmed after hearing a scraped plate. "Are you moving here permanently?"

Bree laughed. "Oh, no. My parents have a summer cottage here—"

"I agreed to show her the nontouristy places before she leaves," Darren interrupted.

"I gotta run." Cam skipped down the steps. "Nice to see you again, Bree."

His mom didn't let it go. "What kind of places?"

"We went smelt dipping with Kate and Neil on Friday." This conversation was taking an odd turn, and Darren wanted it back on track.

"How'd you do?" His dad's eyes lit up. "I haven't been dipping in years."

"We got close to our limits." Darren scanned the streets. An old man walked his dog. Churchgoers heading home. No one to worry about.

"I've never done anything like that before, and it was fun," Bree added.

"You poor thing." Monica laughed. "Darren's more at home outside than in. I've gotta run. Chamber meeting with Brady."

"On Sunday?" Darren knew it didn't matter the day. His sister had had a crush on the chamber of commerce president for a while now. The guy didn't know what he was in for. Or maybe he did, and that's why he'd never asked Monica out.

"As good a day as any other." Monica got all prickly as if daring him to make something of it.

He raised his hands in surrender. "Fine."

"Good," Monica sparred back.

His mom intervened. "Come on, let's go where it's warm instead of clogging up the church steps."

"Bye." Monica elbowed him in the ribs before bolting. "Nice."

Bree glanced at him. Looking uncomfortable. Maybe she didn't want to go and couldn't say no.

Darren knew how she felt. His mom was a formidable force. In fact, his entire family could be intimidating because of the sheer number of them. "If you're busy—"

"No, no plans right now." Bree kicked at the sidewalk.

"Let's go, then." Darren gestured for her to walk next to him.

They followed his parents down the block and turned toward the diner. His mom stopped when they came to his brother's glass shop. "My eldest son, Zach, owns this store."

Bree peeked inside the window decorated with blown glass ornaments of all shapes and sizes. "I heard about this place from Stella. She loves it."

"He's closed on Sundays, but have Darren bring you in for a tour," his mom offered.

"I'll have to stop in regardless." Bree pulled back from the window and they resumed walking. "How many brothers and sisters do you have?"

"Six and three."

Bree gave him a wide-eyed look. "And I thought it was bad with only one sister to drive me nuts."

Darren chuckled. "You don't get along?"

"We do. It's just that, well, she's the one who did everything right. While I…"

"You what?"

Bree shrugged, looking uncomfortable again. "I'm still finding my way."

Darren's arm brushed against Bree's, and it seemed natural to take hold of her hand. She didn't pull away. Her hand felt small in his, delicate. The pads of her fingers were tough. Those calluses proved her strength. Bree didn't give herself enough credit.

He looked down at her and smiled.

She smiled back.

What was he doing? This sure felt like the start of a relationship hanging out with his folks. Bree must have felt it, too, because she looked thoughtful. Maybe her hesitation in accepting the invitation to breakfast was wrapped up in how right it felt to hold her hand. How right *they* felt together.

He let go. "So, were you just out walking?"

"Yes. After church I like to walk and meditate on the message, you know? Let it sink in."

"Huh." Darren couldn't remember this morning's sermon. He held open the door to the tiny restaurant that served only breakfast and lunch.

A staple in town for plain home cooking, Dean's Hometown Grille had been owned by the same woman for years. Once inside, Darren was hit with the familiar smell of strong coffee, cinnamon rolls and bacon grease. It had been a while.

They grabbed a booth, and Darren let Bree slide in first. His mom watched his every move as if he might fall and she wanted to be there to catch him. He wasn't five. At thirty-five, Darren was old enough to learn from his mistakes. He hoped Bree wouldn't be one of them.

Linda, the owner, delivered four water-filled glasses. She pulled an order pad from the pocket of her red-checkered apron and a pencil from the bun of her gray hair. "Well, I'll be. Darren Zelinsky, I thought maybe you'd moved away."

"Never." He smiled.

Linda, as well as half of Maple Springs, knew why he'd stayed away from town. It was no secret that Raleigh and Tony lived in a posh apartment overlooking the public beach.

Linda gave him a friendly pat. "Good to have you back. Now, what can I get you?"

After giving their orders, Darren shifted, all too aware of Bree, who'd wedged herself into the corner to give him plenty of room. He heard her stomach rumble and chuck-led. "Hungry?"

"Starved."

Proof that her hesitation to join them hadn't been about her appetite. "Ever been here before?"

"Once with my father, but my mother thinks the food is too greasy for anyone's good."

"Don't let Linda hear you."

"I'll remember that." Bree sipped her water.

"What kind of things are you interested in seeing while you're here?" Darren's mom got down to business.

"It all started with the wild edibles class. Roaming the woods is a novel experience for me."

His mom glanced at him.

"She's a cellist heading to Seattle in a few weeks for two years," Darren explained.

"With a symphony?" His mom looked even more im-pressed as Bree filled her in. "Oh, I'd love to hear you play."

Their breakfasts arrived. "Let's pray." Darren's father said the blessing before digging in.

"Well, I'm playing in a string quartet for the Mother's Day brunch at the Maple Springs Inn."

His mom looked at him. "Oh, Darren, we should go."

Not a chance. "Maybe."

"If you're looking to try new things, you should come by the sugar shack and check out our maple syrup," his dad offered.

"You make maple syrup?" Bree had that kid-in-a-candy-store look in her eyes. The same look she'd had when she spotted her first morel and scooped up her first net of smelt.

He liked that expression. Maybe too much. It made him

want to show her things that would make her look like that again. And again.

"You'll have to come out and see. We had an excellent harvest of sap this year," his mom added.

"Oh, I'd love to."

"Then we'll set a date. And maybe you can bring your cello. We'll make you play for syrup. How's that?"

Bree laughed. "That sounds wonderful."

Darren concentrated on his biscuits and gravy. He was sunk. Bringing Bree to his parents' smacked of a romantic relationship. But then, he'd held Bree's hand while they walked here. What was that? "Maybe we can make a class out of it."

His mother nodded. "Sure. Your dad would love to give a tour, and there are morels in the woods. When do you want to do this?"

"How about a week from this Tuesday? We were going to look for white morels anyway. Might as well scour our own woods." Darren liked this idea. There'd be protection in numbers. It'd be a work-related outing. That's all it'd be.

That's what he'd make it.

Tuesday afternoon, Bree growled when her phone whistled with an incoming text interrupting her cello practice. If it was Philip after she'd told him to stop, she'd scream. Laying aside her bow, she grabbed the phone and her breath caught.

It was Darren.

I've got your sweater. Will bring to class.

She ran her finger over the screen and texted back.

Thanks. See you later this afternoon.

He didn't reply. There was no need.

She tipped her head back and closed her eyes. Darren couldn't be labeled a charmer, but there was something about him—something unsettling in how a simple thing like holding his hand had turned her upside down. Maybe she should look at him like a test that needed passing, proving her resolve. Was God testing her?

She'd almost let Philip talk her out of applying for the music residency. He'd said she wasn't good enough because she didn't play in the top-tier, more prestigious orchestras. It wasn't as if she didn't worry about that same thing, but she'd get nowhere if she didn't try. A man worth his salt wouldn't hold her back. He'd encourage her to reach her potential.

What kind of man was Darren?

Taking up her bow, Bree practiced. She played classics, she played modern pieces, even one of her own compositions, but her thoughts kept wandering toward today's class. Scouring the woods for ramps and fiddleheads promised adventure. And dirt.

When she finally glanced at the clock on the stand next to her bed, she had to hurry to pack her cello into its case. She slipped on a pair of thick socks, followed by the hiking boots she'd purchased. Next she threw on a thick fleece shirt and over that her gold windbreaker, a hat and gloves and headed downstairs.

"Your practice sounded good, Bree." Her mother was bundled up on the couch with a throw blanket.

The gas fireplace hummed instead of snapping and crackling with real fire. The carefully controlled flames twisted inside a fake log cage, giving off only a modest amount of heat. Bree stared at it, lost for a moment. It did the job but was nothing special. Clean and convenient.

Easy to flip a switch instead of working hard for the real thing.

Bree wanted real fire in her life. Would Seattle provide it?

"Did you hear me?"

Bree shook loose her thoughts. "What?"

"You okay, honey? You're not coming down with something, are you? This cottage is drafty, and with cold weather like this, it's a wonder both of us aren't sick."

Bree smiled. "I'm fine. I'm heading out for class."

"Let me know how it goes. I heard pretty good feedback overall, but—"

"But what?"

Her mother clicked her tongue. "Ed thinks this DNR guy is a know-it-all."

Bree laughed out loud. "How well do you know Ed?"

She smiled, understanding her meaning. "Well enough, I suppose. Even so—"

"Don't worry. I'll give you a full report." Bree grabbed a basket and left.

Ed. What a character. Maybe she should tell Darren. But to what end? She didn't want to cause any rifts or trouble. Maybe it'd be better to let it go for now and see how things went. Darren had already proved he could handle someone like Ed.

Ten minutes later, when she walked into the community room, Darren greeted her with a ready smile. "Glad to see you dressed warm. With this cold snap, we might have a light group."

His wide smile turned her inside out. Not good.

Bree set down her basket and lifted her foot onto the chair with a clunk. "Check these out."

Darren laughed. "Good job on the boots. I have your

sweater in the van. You might need the extra layer. It's cold."

"I think I'll be okay."

She heard Stella's voice followed by several others as people arrived. After waiting only a few minutes, Bree knew Darren was surprised when everyone showed, bundled up and with baskets in hand. Even Ed, who grumbled about the weather, seemed eager to go.

In no time, they loaded up into the van and set out. Bree sat in the passenger seat again. Everyone else had slipped into the same seats as last week. "Where to? Same woods?"

"No." Darren took a turn and headed south, and then took another turn eastward according to the compass on the dash. "Different land. Loaded with trillium and ramps. And further in are fiddleheads. I've found them there before."

Bree had heard of fiddleheads when she'd traveled out east.

She and Philip had gone with her parents to Vermont one spring weekend for a fine art show. Her folks had come home with a prized painting. Bree had returned with yet another reason why Philip wasn't right for her. At the bed-and-breakfast where they'd stayed, Bree had wanted to try fiddleheads. Philip had given her so much grief about eating something that grew like a weed that she finally gave up. She didn't bother ordering any and missed her opportunity to try something new. Something different.

She'd always given in instead of standing her ground. Today she'd look for fiddleheads, and if she found some, she'd eat them. But ramps she wasn't familiar with.

"What are ramps?" she asked.

"They're a wild leek and taste like a cross between an onion and garlic."

"Oh." Simple.

After a few twists and turns on what Darren called "seasonal roads," and more bumps and jostling that led to laughter, they finally came to a stop. Bree got out and looked around. These woods were dense. The ground was covered with white trillium flowers, and a few purple ones dotted the carpet of white.

"Beautiful." She breathed in the cold spring air, feeling a zip of boldness. She felt alive. More alive than ever before.

"Remember, ladies, no picking the trillium. They are protected plants." Darren opened the doors at the back of the vehicle. "Please gather round the van for instruction and tools."

"Ooh, tools. What did you bring?" Stella tried to peek over his shoulder but couldn't.

"Small planting shovels for loosening the soil around the ramps." Darren stepped aside. "Grab a whistle lanyard along with a shovel. Remember to stay in pairs. If you get turned around—"

"We know—use the whistle and you'll find us." Ed's voice dripped sarcasm.

Bree glanced at Darren.

He took it in stride. "Right. And if you'll look at the book on page five…"

They were already wandering away.

"Come on, folks, let's stay together." Darren kept his voice even, but several ignored him and kept walking.

Bree gathered her courage and blew her whistle. Hard. "Don't you want to know what we're looking for?"

Everyone stopped. Darren jiggled his finger in his ear as if she'd blown out his hearing. "Thanks, I think."

Stella grinned at her. "She's right. Get back here, Ed. Connie. Let's find out what they look like."

"I know what they look like," Ed spat back.

"Then we'll follow you." Darren slipped the edibles booklet back into the pocket of his official-looking canvas jacket.

He seemed calm, but Bree felt tension in him. And she noticed that the tops of his ears were red. This man held back his anger instead of giving it full vent. He had control.

"But we'll meet at the van in twenty minutes and move to the next spot." Darren's stern voice warned against argument.

Ed gave him a nod.

Bree wasn't sure why Ed wanted to challenge Darren, but at least the class was moving toward a clump of green leaves with purplish stems that disappeared into the dirt.

"These are wild leeks," Ed said and waited.

"Correct." Darren bent and used his garden shovel to pry around them, loosening the dirt and bringing up slender white bulbs at the end of those pink-purple stems. "And that's all there is to it."

"Wow, easy. And look how many there are." Connie scanned the area.

"I'm thinking of a potato-leek soup recipe I have." Stella took Bree's hand. "Come with me. We'll have a bunch in no time."

Bree laughed. The tense moment was forgotten as everyone spread out and started digging up ramps. An oniony scent filled the air along with everyone's chatter. She spotted Darren on his cell phone, so at least they had coverage out here. Bree had turned hers off.

"Did you enjoy smelt dipping?" Stella asked.

"I did." The fingertips of Bree's gloves were crusted with dirt. She should have grabbed her mom's garden variety instead of these knitted ones.

"And?" Stella wiggled her eyebrows.

Bree glanced at Darren, who was out of earshot, digging up a few ramps of his own. "And nothing. He's a nice guy and so are his friends."

"But?"

Brec appreciated her elderly friend's attempt at kind matchmaking, but it was a moot point. "I'm leaving soon, remember? I can't get involved."

"You like him—"

"As a friend, Stella. As a friend." Bree needed to keep that in mind. She didn't know what the next two years held but knew she had to go. God had given her this opportunity, maybe to find real purpose. She needed fire in her life, not convenient settling for the easier route. Falling for Darren might be easy and full of exciting fire, but living here would be neither. What could she really do here with her music?

Twenty minutes went by fast, and Bree's basket was indeed full when she heard Darren announce they needed to load up.

No one had ventured far, so they quickly climbed in the van. Darren headed deeper into the woods, bouncing along an even rougher road. The surrounding trees thinned, and scrubby pines popped up along with mounds of old brown ferns. A creek sliced through a small field with twists and turns.

"Wow, we're really out here." Bree had no idea where they were. She exited the van with the rest of the group, anxious to find these elusive fiddleheads.

Darren got out too, and scowled. "Okay, folks, let's stick close. The weather's going to turn."

Bree looked up. Sure enough, dark clouds had rolled in and the temperature had dropped. The light gurgling sound of that creek reminded her of smelt fishing and cold water, making her shiver. She blew her breath out in long white tendrils of mist. "It's really cold."

"That's snow." Darren had everyone's attention as he nodded toward the clouds.

"You're kidding." Bree looked up. "But it's May."

"Let's make this quick, before we all freeze." Stella stamped her feet. At least everyone had the sense to wear boots and coats. Not everyone wore hats and gloves, though.

"That okay with everyone?" Darren asked. "Ed?"

"If we must." He looked like he'd sucked on a sour lemon.

"Yup," Connie said.

"Your call," the other elderly gentleman agreed.

Darren went over what they were looking for in the booklet and then elaborated. "There will be several fronds, or fiddleheads, shooting up from the base. Pick only three, and leave the rest so we don't kill the plant. Look for a brown papery coating. I'll try to find the first one, but it's anyone's game here. If you do find one, whistle so we can all see it."

They split up with instructions to meet back at the van in twenty minutes.

Of course, Darren found the first one. "Right here, folks. This is a fiddlehead. And there are several more along there, toward the creek."

Bree forgot all about the cold, jogged toward a field filled with them and picked. Only three per plant. Bree hoped everyone else followed the rules. The immature ferns were a pretty spring green with a grassy scent. Delicate. Wild. She'd try these and find out what she'd missed out on in Vermont.

She made room in her basket for the fiddleheads when the first snowflake fell. Another, and then another. Bree pulled out her phone and took a picture of her basket of

goodies with fat snowflakes nestled amid the greens before they melted.

She looked up and noticed that everyone had already
gathered around the van. With a sigh, she picked up her
basket and walked back. The snow fell heavier now. The
flakes stuck to her eyelashes. But it was beautiful and
quiet. So very quiet.

At the van, she noticed a hush had settled over all of
them as they stood and watched it snow across a pretty
field filled with fiddleheads near a small stream.

Darren did a head count. "Where's Connie?"

Bree looked at Stella. And everyone looked at Ed.

"She wasn't with me." Ed raised his hands in surrender.
"I'm not her keeper."

Bree glanced at Darren.

"Everyone get in the van and stay there. I'll do a quick
sweep."

"Can I help?" Bree asked.

"Stay in the van." Darren gave her a nod. "Keep them
in there, Bree."

She nodded. He didn't need more people getting lost.
Not out in weather like this. She flicked on her phone—
still bars but only a couple in this spot.

"Come on, let's do what he said and get in the van. We'll
be warmer in there." She hoped that proved true, because
Darren hadn't left her the keys.

She watched him disappear over a small hill. They were
on their own, but then, so was Connie.

Chapter Seven

Darren walked a large half circle, calling out Connie's name to no avail. The snow fell and stuck in places. A snowy ground cover would soon mask tracks, making his search more difficult. He'd started by following many sets of footprints that had become a few and then one. Someone had walked this way. He hoped it was Connie.

He shuddered to think what might happen if she kept moving, wandering farther away. He hoped she had sense enough to stop and wait, knowing they'd look for her, but the fact that she hadn't blown her whistle worried him. What if she'd fallen? With an older woman, that was all too possible. Add in the temperature drop, and he had to find her—fast.

He checked his watch. He'd been searching fifteen minutes with no success. He prayed everyone stayed in that van.

His cell phone buzzed with an incoming text message. From Bree.

Connie is here. Safe and sound.

Darren texted back.

Good. Be there shortly.

Shaking his head, he made his way back. Spotting a small red thing sticking out of the snow at the base of a tree, Darren knew why Connie hadn't used her whistle. He stooped over and picked it up. The string of the lanyard was broken.

Nice. He gritted his teeth. She'd have had access to another whistle if she'd stayed in a pair as he'd instructed.

Darren rubbed his forehead. But then, he'd rushed them with the threat of snow. He'd counted all of them in the field, and then his attention had snagged on Bree taking pictures of her basket. Was that when Connie had wandered off?

This incident wasn't going to look good to Bree's mom. Nor did he look forward to entering it in his daily field report, but he wouldn't shirk his duties. Connie's mishap was his own fault. He was dealing with older people who needed reminding to stay in pairs because of the dangers out here. Many of the missing person searches he'd been part of had found folks a mile or less from where they'd started out.

He'd do better. Blowing out his breath, Darren made quick time back to the van. The windows were steamed up with so many in there. He noticed Bree's passenger window and one in the back had been rolled down some to let in fresh air. Smart girl.

Without a word, he climbed in the driver's side, started the van and cranked up the front and rear defrosters.

"Darren, I'm so sorry," Connie said.

"Not much of a tracker, are you?" Ed sneered.

"Ed—" Bree and Stella chorused together, ready to jump all over the guy.

Darren raised his hand to quiet everyone, then turned and faced them. "All the more reason to stay in pairs. Got it?"

He looked at Connie. She held something in her hand besides her basket of ramps and fiddleheads. She'd picked a couple of jack-in-the-pulpits. Those wildflowers, which happened to be protected on state lands, were the reason she'd veered away from the group.

Staring down Ed, he reiterated the seriousness of the situation. "Let's use this as a reminder of how easy it is to get turned around out here. Agreed?"

"Absolutely, Darren." Stella led the group in agreement.

Even Ed nodded, but he didn't look impressed.

Darren didn't care. The old guy was impossible to please. He'd encountered Ed's type several times in the woods, especially during hunting season. Men who weren't going to let the DNR tell them how to do things.

He glanced at Connie, and the woman looked so forlorn that Darren gave her an encouraging smile. At least she'd apologized instead of giving him that air of snobbishness he expected from Bay Willows residents. It dawned on him that there wasn't much of that with this group. Not much at all.

He'd bust her about those flowers, but only a warning. It'd be bad form to ticket one of his class attendees.

"Okay, let's get back to town." He didn't say any more but glanced at Bree.

She gave him a proud smile. She had his back.

He could count on her, and that realization broke something deep inside. She'd chiseled a hole in the shell he'd built around his heart. A year and a half of careful construction, and Bree had rammed through with one look, one smile. Dangerous, maybe, but it felt good.

Bree stayed behind to help Darren clean up the community room kitchen from their preparations of fiddleheads and ramps. She'd finally tried them, and while the ramps were super flavorful, the fiddleheads didn't live up to all the hype.

"Could you introduce me to your mom?" Darren dried off the frying pan and placed it in the cupboard.

Bree stopped wiping off the counter. "Yeah, sure. What's up?"

Darren looked pensive. "I'd like to let her know what happened today. I'd rather she didn't hear it secondhand."

From her. Is that what he meant? Bree nodded. "Sure, we can walk over there right now."

"I'll drive."

It wasn't far. Was it meeting her mother that had Darren looking so uncomfortable? Silly. Her parents were nice people. Although her father wasn't around. He'd returned home in order to work in Detroit for the week. They exited the building and climbed back into the van.

"Where should I go?"

"Drive straight for two blocks and take a left toward the lake." Bree pointed. "We're on the corner in a white cottage with green trim."

When he didn't say anything, Bree tried to lighten the mood a little. "She won't bite."

Darren tipped his head. "Who?"

"My mother. She's a reasonable woman. Well, most of the time."

He chuckled. "It's not that." He pulled in front of her parents' cottage and stared out over the bay.

Small, insignificant snowflakes fell and disappeared as soon as they hit the ground. Nothing like the heavier snow they'd had earlier while on state land.

Bree waited.

He shrugged. "There are a lot of memories here."

"Of Raleigh?"

Darren nodded.

"What happened?" Bree knew what Kate had said, and Stella, too, but Bree wanted to know why. Maybe Darren didn't know the answer to that. "I mean, if you care to share."

He looked at her. "It's old news. I can't believe you didn't hear about it. She took off with my best man the night before our wedding, right after rehearsal."

Hearing him say it in such a matter-of-fact way made her wince because of the pain in his eyes. This was a wound that still festered. "I'm so sorry."

"In hindsight, we probably wouldn't have worked." He made a sweeping gesture. "I can't provide all this."

"This?" Bree didn't miss the bitterness in his voice.

"I live a simple life and I like it that way."

Bree felt her hackles go up when she remembered Neil's comment about Darren's dislike of the summer resorters. "Not everyone who comes up here is a jerk, you know. This isn't *Lifestyles of the Rich and Famous*. We're just people who've made a tradition of summering here."

"People with a lot more cash than I'll ever have." Darren didn't sound envious at all, just disappointed. As if the summer community had let him down.

Was that because of Raleigh? Or a pattern of actions by some of the more arrogant wannabes who also summered here? She'd run into a few of them, too, but that didn't mean she painted everyone with the same broad stroke.

Her parents had pushed Philip with her because of the security his career provided. They wanted her settled with the promise of being taken care of. She'd grown up with an expectation of financial security, and maybe too much emphasis was made on that sort of stability.

By accepting the music residency, Bree had placed her trust in God's provision. She had faith that she'd find the right path through this opportunity, but it wasn't about the money. Her music had never been about the money.

"Come on, then. I'll show you how the other half lives." She gave him a smirk.

He laughed, getting the joke, and his tension eased.

They weren't rich. Very few in Bay Willows could have been called seriously wealthy, but many were secure or they couldn't have maintained two homes. Many of the cottages here had been handed down and kept in the family. A long-standing tradition of summering up north in a beautiful place that was void of the employment options found elsewhere.

Bree glanced at Darren as he walked up her parents' porch steps. The man oozed a different kind of security. A woman could depend on him to do the right thing. That kind of stability was harder to find. That kind of strength lasted.

She slipped past him, walked inside, set down her basket of edibles and pulled off her hat and windbreaker. "Would you like something to drink? Coffee? Or pop?"

"No. I'm good." He looked determined and a little antsy.

"I can take your coat."

He refused that, too. "I won't be long."

Of course not. He didn't want to socialize with her kind. Now who was the snob? Bree nearly laughed at the thought. She brought him into the living room, where her mother sat in a wingback chair with her foot propped up on an ottoman stacked with pillows. "Mom, this is Darren Zelinsky, the conservation officer facilitating your class."

Her mother glanced over the rim of her reading glasses, and then her face brightened into a smile. She reached out her hand. "Nice to meet you. Sorry, I'd get up, but I just got situated."

Darren returned the handshake. "No problem, Mrs. Anderson. I thought I'd touch base and let you know how your class is progressing."

"Wonderful. Please, sit down, and call me Joan."

Darren did as asked but didn't relax. He leaned forward, bracing his elbows on his knees. "Today we had an incident I wanted you to be aware of."

Concern flashed across her mother's face. "What happened?"

Bree sat down, too, but kept quiet.

"One of the ladies got turned around in the woods. It could have been a bad situation, especially with this weather, but fortunately, she found her way back before too long. She'd lost her whistle and veered away from her partner. We have to stay in pairs."

Bree watched her mother digest that information, feeling like a school-age kid sitting in on a parent-teacher conference.

"Yes, of course." Her mother nodded agreement and glanced at her. "Bree, was there anything you could have done to prevent this?"

Bree had been caught with her head in the clouds once again. She opened her mouth, but Darren cut her off before she could speak.

"Your daughter has been a big help, but keeping everyone safe is my responsibility."

Her mother's eyes narrowed. "Thank you for telling me. I'll be walking with only a cane in a couple days, so I should be able to join you for the next class."

"About that." Darren pulled out the schedule from inside his jacket. "My parents have offered to give a tour of their maple syrup operation, and their nearby woods should be loaded with tan and white morels, so I've made that change."

"Wonderful. That works very well."

"Good." Darren rose to his feet. "I won't keep you. Thank you, Joan."

"I'll walk you out." Bree led Darren back out onto the front porch. "Thanks for that, but you didn't have to come to my rescue."

"I stated a fact. I'm responsible for everyone in that class."

"Yeah, but if I hadn't been taking pictures, I might have seen Connie wander off." She rubbed her arms.

"They're adults, Bree. And old enough to follow instructions. Instructions made clear that first day." His voice softened. "Do you think your mom is okay with that?"

Bree nodded. Surely this wouldn't impact the promotion he was after. It wasn't his fault Connie wandered away.

"You should go inside. It's cold out here."

Bree still felt like she'd failed him somehow. "Okay. See you next week?"

"Next week. And be sure to bring your cello. My mom wants to hear you play."

"Why not take her to brunch on Mother's Day? I'm playing in a string quartet."

He got a funny look on his face. "I don't really do that sort of thing."

Bree laughed. "Yeah, well, I don't smelt dip either, and I found out that I liked it. A lot."

His blue eyes looked uncertain, thoughtful. "I'll think about it."

"Do that." Bree had expected him to decline outright, but he didn't, and that made her smile. She had a hunch he'd be there.

She watched him climb into the van and waved as he pulled out.

He waved back.

She sighed and headed inside.

Her mother was up with her crutches, waiting for her. "Bree, what's going on? What was that all about?"

"Darren wanted you to hear about Connie getting lost from him. It wasn't a big deal. Connie found her way back in like ten minutes."

Her mother watched her closely.

"What?"

"Darren is a handsome man." Her mother made it sound like some huge problem.

"So?"

Her mother's gaze bore into hers. "So, you're spending a lot of time with him. Why?"

"We're just friends."

She didn't believe that for an instant.

"This is my vacation, Mom. Maybe the last one for a long time. Darren's showing me around because I've never been anywhere up here. He's fun and that's it. Nothing to worry about."

"Okay." Her mother didn't question her further. She peeked in the basket of ramps and fiddleheads. "Let's see what we can make for dinner with what you brought home this week."

Bree breathed easier, but a knot settled between her shoulder blades. One she'd have to stretch out before she practiced her cello. She didn't want anything more than friendship with Darren. Sure, she had a bit of a crush on him, but that was no doubt temporary. As her mother had pointed out, he was a handsome man. Who wouldn't find him attractive?

That didn't mean she'd let this attraction grow into something that'd knock her off track. Bree had hit the snooze button on her biological clock because a husband and kids were quicksand. She had plenty of years yet, but for the first time in a long while, she considered the tick of that internal clock. Darren struck her as the kind of guy who'd want kids. What if he was that someone special she'd miss out on to pursue her dreams.

Bree wanted no more regrets.

She'd dated Philip on and off for close to two years, and she'd known him for years before that. It had taken her forever to figure out finally that he wasn't right for her. After only a couple of weeks, how could she even consider Darren a candidate for life?

Engaged after only a month.

Bree had thought that kind of thing ridiculous before a pair of bright blue eyes made almost anything seem possible. And completely impossible.

His day off and Darren sat at his dining room table entering the last few days' worth of field reports. Bree's words rang through his thoughts. *They're just people.*

Covering what had happened to Connie in his report made him think long and hard. When push came to shove, Bree was right. They were just people who summered here. They got lost and made mistakes like anyone else. There was no reason to treat them differently.

Growing up, he'd hated that many who summered here acted like they somehow owned Maple Springs. Sure, every merchant depended on the summer crowd spending dollars to survive. The entire town looked for ways to make Maple Springs more attractive to tourists. More wasn't always better. He might live way out in the woods, but Maple Springs was his hometown and he wanted to protect it. It was the reason he'd gone for the supervisor position a couple of years ago, only to come in second. Had he been overlooked because of his attitude toward the tourists?

He ran his hands through his hair and then stretched.

Bree's sweater, folded as neatly as he could manage, lay at the end of the table. She'd forgotten to grab it from the van the other day, so he brought it back inside where it would stay clean. He wouldn't know how to wash something delicate like that. He'd probably ruin it.

He'd ruin a lot of things if he let his feelings for Bree get out of hand before she left.

He looked out his windows, where the sun shone and the temperatures had climbed back toward spring. He had a dozen things to do but didn't want to. Neil was at work, and his brothers were, too. Well, not Cam. On this Friday afternoon, Darren wanted to go somewhere. He didn't care where as long as he was with Bree.

His beagles snoozed on the floor in a puddle of sunshine streaming in through the windows.

The forecast called for climbing temperatures into the weekend and beyond. The elk would be moving today after the cold snap, no doubt getting out into the meadows to graze on the new growth.

He glanced at Bree's sweater, grabbed his phone and texted her.

Are you busy?

After a few seconds he got a text back.

Practicing. What's up?

He typed.

Want to see the elk?

YES!

He smiled. She was easy to please. Another difference from his ex and pretty much every other woman he'd dated. There was a sense of wonder in Bree he liked bringing out. It had nothing to do with tangible gifts. He simply showed her what he loved about Northern Michigan and she responded in kind. Like a real friend would, with no expectations or pressure for more.

Only, he wanted more.

Ignoring the warning bells in his head, he texted back.

I'll pick you up in half an hour.

Great. I'll be home. And bring my sweater. LOL.

He chuckled as he pocketed his phone, shut down his laptop and gathered up her sweater. He brought it to his nose, but her soft floral scent had long since worn off.

Grabbing two harnesses with leashes, he said, "Come on, dogs. Let's go for a ride."

Mickey and Clara perked their ears, but that was it. Neither moved. It had been a long while since he'd taken them for a ride in the truck.

He slapped a hand against his thigh. "Come on, I mean it."

They got up quick and shot past him, down the stairs.

Darren loaded his truck with a blanket across the backseat while his dogs did their business. Then they all climbed in and headed for Maple Springs. Less than twenty minutes later, he pulled near the driveway of the Anderson cottage and glanced out over the bay. The water looked aqua followed by the deeper blue of an open Lake Michigan beyond.

Bree stood outside on the porch. She shifted a backpack over her shoulder and ran toward his truck. She laughed when both beagles stuck their heads out the window, begging for pats. She obliged them. "You brought your dogs."

"There are some nice walking trails in the Pigeon River Forest."

"I've got my hiking boots on, so I'm ready." She also wore khaki shorts and an expensive brand-name black pullover with a white T-shirt underneath. Her hair hung in two long braids, making her look like a Girl Scout who knew her way around. The red lipstick was a dead giveaway that she didn't.

"What's with the pack?"

She climbed into his truck. "Just some recording stuff."

He spotted Joan at the window and gave her a wave.

She waved back but had a pinched look on her face. He didn't need Bree's mom getting weird about him going out with her daughter. Maybe Joan always looked like that, but Darren knew better. He'd seen that kind of look many times in his life. She gave him the perfect Bay Willows cold stare.

"Is your mom okay with you doing this?"

Bree set her pack on the floor at her feet and waved off his question. "It's not like I need her permission—"

"Right." Stupid question to ask. Darren looked at her backpack. "What's the recording stuff for?"

"To record what I hear out there. Why aren't you working today?"

His turn to explain. "I worked last night."

Worry flashed quick across her face. "What'd you do?"

"Had to check out a complaint of ORVs tearing around after dark."

"ORVs?"

"Off-road vehicles. A couple of guys were riding four-wheelers on the walking trails where they shouldn't have."

Bree's eyes grew round as golden marbles. "What happened?"

"I issued them tickets."

"Were they mad?"

Darren chuckled. "They weren't happy."

"Are you ever afraid? I mean, you're out there by yourself, right?"

"Yeah, but most folks are just out to have fun. On occasion they get out of hand. Or don't have the proper registration or licensing. Usually it all goes fine."

"What if it doesn't?"

Darren turned and headed south. "I call for backup if needed."

"Oh." She bit her lip. "Have you ever had to do that?"

"Sure, yeah." Darren didn't want to get into the dangers he faced. For the most part, people didn't do much more than mouth off. But there'd been moments when Darren wasn't sure what might happen. Moments when he'd had to confront men with weapons hunting illegally.

The key was never letting his guard down and preparing for the worst. He had over ten years of experience under his belt. Teri had over fifteen when she'd transferred in as his immediate supervisor. She was seasoned, knowledgeable and used to working more populated areas than Darren. Another Teri could be vying for the same position he wanted.

"How often do you have to do that?"

He shrugged. "If we're investigating a big poaching ring or something, we'll work in pairs. Call in the supervisor or sometimes team up with the county sheriff's department. I stay safe."

Bree looked scared. For him.

He didn't want that. At least with her, he already knew the worst case scenario. She'd leave for a long time. Too long to make something more with her. No matter how much he liked hanging out with her, he needed to keep his guard up. The guard she kept climbing over.

He changed the subject. "So tell me, what do you want to record?"

She brightened. "Things like the breeze through the trees, maybe even the sound of elk. Do they make much noise?"

Darren chuckled. "Not now. But during mating season in the fall, the males make a big show, bellowing and shaking trees with their antlers in order to impress the females."

"Wow. That must be something. Funny how God instills that competitive drive in animals."

"People, too." Darren wanted that promotion. He'd do everything he could to make sure this time, he got it.

"Yeah, but maybe we compete for the wrong reasons."

He looked at her. "What makes you say that?"

"Oh, I don't know. Have you ever second-guessed why you wanted something?" Bree clicked on the radio, and a soft country song about unrequited love spilled out.

"Not until she took off."

Bree chuckled. "That sounds bitter."

He shrugged. "It is what it is. Are you having doubts about going to Seattle?"

"No. I don't know. Maybe. What if I'm not good enough?"

Darren glanced her way. He knew all about those kinds of thoughts. Driving across the country by herself to start a new life took guts. Her desire to conquer what lay off the beaten path suddenly made a lot of sense. This woman was scared. For all the right and wrong reasons. "You wouldn't have been chosen unless you were good enough."

Bree smiled, making those dimples tease him. "The same can be said of you. Raleigh's the one who made the mistake by walking away."

"Hmm." Darren focused on the road ahead.

It was a compliment he didn't want to hear, especially from a woman who'd do the same thing.

Chapter Eight

Bree looked out the window, in awe of the various shades of green displayed from new leaves to rich grass and dark evergreens. Darren drove slowly along an unpaved road through a stretch of open fields. His dogs hung their heads out the back windows, sniffing the fresh air.

"What do they smell, do you think?"

"All kinds of game. Squirrel, deer, elk."

Bree inhaled a hint of pine and decayed leaves as they drove over a small branch.

"It might have been a bad idea to bring the dogs. If we see elk, they're bound to bark."

Bree looked in the back and smiled. "I'm glad you brought them. They look happy."

He chuckled. "Wait till we're walking."

Bree could relate. This felt a whole lot like unworried freedom. "Thanks for bringing me out here."

"No problem." He concentrated on turning onto another trail through a thicket of scrubby pine. Then he reached into the glove box and pulled out a couple of dog chew bones that he gave to Mickey and Clara before raising the back windows. He slowed to a stop and pointed. "See there, through those trees?"

Bree matched his near whisper. "Where?" An elk stepped from behind a cluster of bushes, followed by another one and another. "Oh. Wow."

"Yeah."

They watched in silence as the small group of elk lingered, grazing on the new grass poking up through the old. The dogs were busy with their bones and stayed quiet.

Bree glanced at Darren's strong profile. She was tempted to run her fingertip down the straight line of his nose. He hadn't shaved, and the light stubble along his jawline made her want to find out if those whiskers might be soft or scratchy. She folded her hands in her lap to keep from touching him to find out. Then she said the first thing that popped into her mind. "Where are the babies?"

"Calving starts the end of this month." He pointed. "There's a pregnant cow."

Bree spotted the elk that looked a little fatter than the others, but she'd have never guessed it carried a calf. "Look at that."

"Yeah."

She sensed Darren's gaze and turned.

He looked right at her.

She stared back.

The interior of the truck grew tight. Time had stopped and held its breath, like her. She leaned toward Darren and then hesitated. She didn't dare make that first move. Didn't dare act on the overwhelming desire to kiss this man. Would he push her away? What if he didn't?

One of the dogs barked, a bellowing sound that shattered the moment and made the elk trot off. The other beagle chorused in with a deeper bugling sound.

Bree laughed, even as Darren scolded his dogs to stop. She patted Clara's head, grateful the dog had kept her from making a big mistake. Bree scratched behind the dog's velvet-soft floppy ear. "They're gone, silly."

Darren hushed the dogs again before backing up his truck. "We might as well hit the trailhead and walk."

"That'd be great." Bree couldn't shake the disappointment of not acting on impulse. It would not have been smart to kiss Darren, but it sure felt like she'd missed out yet again.

When they finally parked, Darren quickly hooked up the dogs' leashes and got out. He pulled a couple of water bottles from a small cooler in the open truck bed and handed one to Bree.

"Thanks." She slipped it into an outside pocket of the backpack and then hoisted the whole thing over her shoulders.

"I can carry that."

"It's not heavy." Bree reached toward one of the dogs. "Can I walk one?"

He handed over Mickey. "He likes to stop and sniff, so you'll have to tug him along. No dogs at your house?"

Bree slipped her hand through the handle. "We had a cocker spaniel growing up, but my parents didn't replace her after she died. There was no point with my sister headed for college and me busy with music lessons."

"When did you start playing the cello?" Darren led the way toward the trail.

Bree thought a minute. "I switched from the piano to the cello in fifth grade."

"Why the cello?"

She shrugged. "I liked its sound, but I think it had more to do with hiding behind it. The piano was out there front stage, and as a kid, that was pretty scary."

He gave her a long look.

Bree grinned. "You know, I'm working on that whole bravery thing."

He chuckled. "You're doing a good job."

"Thanks to you."

"Me?" Darren looked appalled, as if he didn't want the responsibility of bringing her out of her shell.

It wasn't all his doing, but he'd certainly helped the process she'd started when she'd mustered the courage to apply for the music residency. She patted his shoulder and felt the muscles tense beneath the fabric of his T-shirt. "You've given me opportunities to stretch. I'm in the middle of the woods and it's all good. I appreciate it."

"You're welcome."

They walked in awkward silence, stopping every so often to let the dogs sniff the ground more thoroughly. Bree kicked herself again for being too afraid to kiss him when the opportunity had presented itself. But then, she had a hunch that kissing Darren might shoot her straight to the moon when she needed to keep her feet firmly planted on the ground.

She glanced at the trees marked with blue paint that guided their steps along a barely discernible trail. The sun's golden rays danced through the spring-green canopy of leaves. Birdsong echoed louder than the breeze gently swishing through the trees. It was beautiful. A perfect composition of beats and chords.

"Can we stop for a bit?"

Darren nodded. "You okay?"

She nodded. "I'd love to record this."

He looked at her as if she were crazy. "Record what?"

"The birdsong, for one. It's so loud."

"Okay, sure." He took Mickey from her.

She slipped off her backpack and opened it. Out came a throw blanket and a recording device hooked to her notebook. While she set everything up, she spotted Darren taking a long swig from his water bottle before offering the rest to his dogs. The beagles lapped at the spout.

"I've never seen a dog drink directly from a water bottle before." Bree knelt on the blanket.

Darren shrugged. "They're used to it. So, what do you have to do here?"

"Just hook up the mic to my notepad and record. Do you mind?"

"Not at all." But he looked hesitant to sit on the blanket.

Bree shifted to sit cross-legged and patted the empty spot next to her. Mickey took that as an invitation to curl onto her lap. She spread her arms wide and smiled. "See? There's plenty of room."

Okay, this is different.

Darren lay on a small stadium blanket, staring at the sky above. His hands were behind his head, and his jeans-clad legs stretched off the blanket onto the ground. Bree's legs did, too. She wore shorts and the grass had to itch, but she hadn't moved.

His dogs made a good barrier, curled between them, sleeping. Darren had never considered the beagles as chaperones, but that's exactly the role they played today, keeping him from taking Bree into his arms. Keeping him out of trouble.

Bree had been serious about recording nature sounds he gave only a passing thought. She'd stayed quiet, listening while recording. If he'd interpreted the half smile on her face correctly, she savored the dee-dee-hum of chickadees, chattering of red squirrels and squawking calls of crows. Nothing exotic. Simple sounds from basic wildlife were considered music to her ears. Surely she could be happy here.

He heard it, too. The music of nature. For once, instead of listening for movement, for voices or law breakers, he lay still and simply listened. Darren shouldn't have felt this comfortable next to a woman like her.

Yawning, he rolled onto his side and looked at her. Really looked at her. Bree's eyes were closed while she stroked Mickey's ears. The beagle rested his head on her midsection, claiming her as his own.

Darren envied his dog. "So, what are you going to do with the recording?"

She didn't open her eyes. "Listen to it and be inspired."

"Inspired?"

Bree sat up and clicked off the recording. She laughed when Mickey readjusted and crawled onto her lap with a contented sigh. "I love this dog."

"I think the feeling is mutual." Darren gave Mickey a scratch behind his ears. "So, back to being inspired—how's that work?"

"I record lots of sounds. I've got traffic recorded from outside my apartment. I've recorded the waves crashing against the shore at my parents' cottage and even crickets chirping from the garage. Anything that might spur ideas for notes, or give me a feeling that I can translate into music on paper or my computer."

"Huh. How much time do you spend between practicing your cello and writing music?"

"Hours and hours."

"You spend a lot of time alone." Not unlike his day of patrolling an area alone and then completing reports from the solitude of his dining room table. Alone.

She shrugged. "Well, yeah, but it's not like I go to a nine-to-five job. Even playing professionally in an orchestra, I worked on my own. We came together to rehearse, but practice is still pretty much a solitary thing, unless I get together with the string section."

Her world was different than his, but similar in some ways. "Right."

Her cell phone buzzed, but she ignored it.

"Aren't you going to check that?"

Bree picked up her phone, glanced at the text and rolled her eyes. "There, checked."

He chuckled. "Telemarketer?"

"No. A family friend." She scrunched up her face. "That's not quite right, either. Philip is a guy I'd been dating until we broke up before I came up north. He wasn't right for me."

"What was wrong with him?" Darren didn't like the idea that she'd had a boyfriend. Up until now he'd thought… He didn't know what he'd thought.

"According to my parents, he's perfect, but he didn't support my decision to accept the music residency, for one thing."

"So you kicked him to the curb."

She chuckled. "That's one way of saying it. Too bad he won't stay on the curb."

"What do you mean?" Darren's voice grew sharp.

"He keeps texting me. He wants to know how I'm doing, as if I'm heartbroken or something." She shrugged. "I don't know. Maybe because I've known him a long time. His parents and mine are friends."

He shouldn't have dug, but something didn't feel right. "How long were you two dating?"

She looked away. "A couple of years, maybe."

Darren's stomach turned. Two years was a long time. Long enough to be considered serious. That guy's frequent texts meant he wanted her back. Plain and simple. Would

Bree take him back? She'd said that her parents wanted them together. That usually pulled weight. A lot of weight.

"We better go." Darren stood.

Bree looked surprised, then disappointed, but she nodded. "Right. Sure."

Darren gathered the leashes of both dogs and pulled them off the blanket so Bree could fold it.

She stashed everything in her pack and shifted it onto her back. She reached out her hand. "Want me to take one?"

He wrestled with an odd notion of protecting Mickey from her heartless abandonment and realized that was crazy. Bree didn't want to go into details about her failed love life any more than he did his. It should have been enough to say that neither of them had worked out.

It wasn't, though. Darren battled a twisted feeling of déjà vu. He didn't like another guy vying for Bree's attention or chasing after her heart.

He handed over the beagle's leash. "Thanks."

They walked back in silence.

At the truck, Bree asked, "Everything okay?"

"Yeah, why?"

"You seem quiet."

He needed to get a grip and grabbed the quickest excuse handy. "Thinking about next week's class. It needs to be good."

"Why wouldn't it be?"

"The morels might be plentiful in the woods at my folks' place, but I want everyone to get enough. Although, there will be a tour of the maple sugar shack. Probably a small jug of syrup, too."

Bree's eyes lit up. "Will we see how the sap is made into syrup?"

Darren shook his head. "Just an explanation. The sap

is collected at the end of March through the first week of April or so. It doesn't keep long and has to be boiled down right away."

"Oh." She looked disappointed again.

Was she really into all this nature stuff? Or was this a way of reeling him in only to cut him loose when it was time for her to leave? Like she'd cut loose a guy she'd been dating for two years. Darren tried to shake off those thoughts. Bree wasn't like that. But then, how'd he know? He'd met her only a week and a half ago.

He loaded up his dogs in the backseat and then climbed in behind the wheel. Glancing at Bree sitting pretty in the passenger seat, he needed a swift kick upside his head. Maybe he hadn't learned his lesson, if he thought he could trust Bree with his heart. He wouldn't be enough for a girl like her.

Thanks again for showing me the elk. It was very inspiring.

Bree sent the text to Darren and waited.

He didn't respond.

She waited a few seconds more. Maybe he was busy. She prayed he was safe, not tracking down some trouble-maker that might turn violent.

She set aside her phone and finished drafting a piece she'd started months ago, at a time when she'd felt stuck. Trapped between Philip's promises and pressure from her parents to get engaged.

God had given her courage then. Courage to see how she'd let everyone else call the shots in her life. Too afraid to step out, she'd settled. Not anymore. Applying for that residency had shifted her thinking and her feelings, too. She wanted more out of life. She wanted fire. Whatever that fire proved to be.

She could easily get burned if she let Darren shift her thinking that they had a future. What would it be like if they had more time to explore the attraction between them? Would they always do these kinds of things, or was he simply showing her a good time as promised before she left?

She felt alive around him. Both comfortable and uncomfortable.

He'd been distant when he drove her home. And she didn't quite buy his excuse about the upcoming class preoccupying his thoughts. Something had changed in him, and she wished she knew what it was.

Her phone whistled with an incoming text.

She reached for it, hesitated a second or two and then clicked open the message.

You're welcome.

Darren had replied with the same sort of to-the-point message she'd come to expect. No smiley faces or anything added on like the texts she sent. Maybe she'd imagined something that wasn't even there. And maybe Tuesday's class couldn't come quickly enough. Unless she saw him sooner, like at the Mother's Day brunch. Closing her eyes, she felt crazy for hoping. Even so, Bree sent a prayer heavenward asking God to guide not only her steps to the future but also her heart. That organ beat to its own tune. One inspired by Darren.

Sunday morning dawned with warmth and sunshine. Darren had driven to his parents' house so he could ride into town with them for church. He'd been roped into attending Mother's Day brunch afterward at the Maple Springs Inn. The place Bree would play. Darren couldn't believe he was here willingly, walking the streets of his hometown as if it didn't matter anymore. Maybe it didn't.

"Thank you for coming. It means a lot to me." His mom looped her arm through his.

"Couldn't let the ticket go to waste." Monica had purchased enough tickets through the chamber of commerce for the whole family to go. As many as were home, anyway. There was no way he could have backed out. Funny thing was, he didn't want to.

"It's a good thing you're not staying away from Maple Springs anymore." His mom patted his arm. "I'm glad you're moving on."

He covered his mom's hand with his own. He wasn't sure about that but gave her the peace she sought. He knew his mom had worried about him. "About time, I suppose."

"To everything there is a season." His mom gripped his hand and squeezed.

"You're right. Seasons come and go." Change was inevitable, but he didn't have to like those changes.

Darren thought more about his mom's reference to the book of Ecclesiastes. *There is a time for everything, and a season for every activity under the heavens.*

He'd been lax in reading his bible for too long, but knew the third chapter of that book pretty well. The simplicity of King Solomon's wise words had always appealed to him.

One verse that came to mind was *a time to weep and a time to laugh.* Bree had helped him with that. Showing her around dispelled a lot of the gloom he'd been under. If today brought him face-to-face with his ex-fiancée, he'd have to deal with it.

A time to keep and a time to throw away.

His time with Bree was limited, only a couple more weeks. Instead of fearing it, maybe he should simply enjoy it. Laugh more and worry less.

Entering the Maple Springs Inn, Darren inhaled the smells of good food and rich coffee. He scanned the fancy lobby with its huge fresh floral displays while they waited in line to enter the dining room. A couple of hours spent here wouldn't kill him. Seeing Raleigh wouldn't, either. Time to let it go. It was time to throw away the bitterness.

"Whoa, Darren, you're here." His brother Matthew carried his wife's tank of a six-month-old baby.

"So are you. When'd you get in?" His brother worked on a Great Lakes freighter and was typically gone this time of year. He leaned toward his sister-in-law for a quick hug. "Morning, Annie. Happy Mother's Day."

"Thanks. Good to see you." She moved on and gave his parents hugs, too.

"I traded shifts so I could be home for this." He nodded toward Annie. "Didn't want to miss her first Mother's Day."

The baby reached toward him, so Darren took the kid from his brother and gave him a friendly bounce. He hadn't seen much of Matthew or Annie since they'd married in February. "Hey, little Jack. What are they feeding you? You're a load."

"He eats everything in sight." Matthew stepped closer. "She's not here, in case you're wondering."

"You've been inside?"

"To ask for a couple of tables put together. Zach and Ginger are coming, Cam, Monica, Marcus, Ben and Erin. Mom would want us sitting together."

"Then I'm glad I came." It wouldn't have been good if he'd missed this. Darren would have been the only local sibling to do so had he not agreed to come. His sister Cat was on assignment somewhere, and his little brother Luke was finishing up his college classes downstate. Both good excuses. Darren's fear of running into his ex-fiancée paled in comparison.

He spotted Bree and openly stared. Dressed in a pretty yellow-print dress with her hair swept up into a swirl at the back of her head, she reminded him of the small yellow trout lilies scattered on the floor of the woods. Sturdy enough to withstand a late snow but too delicate to thrive after being picked. Just like she wouldn't thrive here without a large orchestra to keep her engaged.

Bree saw him and rushed toward him. Her lips were stained the color of ripe berries and more tempting than ever. "You're here!"

"I'm here," he repeated. Holding on to Jack kept Darren from sweeping Bree into his arms.

"And who's this?" She took the baby's hand and laughed when he gurgled at her.

"My nephew, Jack."

Her golden eyes softened into an oddly sappy expression. Even for her.

"What?" he teased.

"Nothing, I—" She looked away. "You're good with him."

"And that surprises you?" Just because he growled about summer residents didn't mean he'd do that to kids. She should see him in action with the area schools. He'd been told his classroom presentations were some of the best.

"Bree." His mom reached for her hands. "I'm looking forward to hearing you play. This is a perfect Mother's Day gift, having most of my kids with me."

Bree's eyes widened, but she smiled. "Darren said he had a big family."

Darren watched, helpless, as his mom introduced her. Every one of his brothers and sisters present looked pointedly at him after hearing her described as *Darren's friend*.

The doors to the dining room finally opened, cutting short the conversation.

"Gotta run. See you inside." Bree gave Jack's chubby hand another playful shake before taking off to disappear down a hallway.

"Who's she?" Matthew asked.

"A friend." Darren shifted the baby to his other arm.

"You sure about that?" Matthew took Jack back as they headed into the dining room.

"I'm not sure of anything anymore."

Matthew gave him a look of understanding. "Give it time."

Time was a luxury he didn't have with Bree.

Their long table had been set up near the windows overlooking the park and Maple Bay. Looking at the public beach with its long stretch of sand and lifeguard chair, Darren recalled the summer that he, his brothers and cousins had *owned* the raft at the edge of the swimming area.

They'd grappled with a group of cocky teens from Bay Willows who'd tried to take over their space. That tussle for turf dominion had resulted in a lifeguard posted on that raft from then on. Sure, a lifeguard might have been a good idea, but it was a sore reminder that what belonged to the locals didn't. Not really. He'd resented the influx of summer residents flooding his town ever since that incident.

He glanced at Bree seated in the corner. Sunshine shimmered in her hair. She didn't take the beauty here for granted. Bree acted more like a guest because, really, that's what she was. She had no permanent roots here.

Bree focused on her sheet music. The cello she played stood nearly as big as she and rested against her knee. Her movements were confident yet refined. Delicate and pretty. She was younger than the three other women playing smaller stringed instruments. The music dipped and swirled and Bree played with an intensity he could relate to. She loved what she did. Not unlike the passion he had for his job and the woods.

She glanced at him and then focused back on the sheets of paper scattered on the stand in front of her. Bree came from a different world than his, with summer homes and prestigious careers, but she seemed to understand him better than most. Certainly, better than Raleigh ever had.

He'd rushed that relationship when he'd had all the time in the world to make sure it was right. He didn't have that kind of time with Bree. Not enough time to trust these new feelings. He'd been wrong before, but could Bree be right—for him?

His youngest sister, Erin, sat next to him and leaned close to whisper, "She's good."

"Huh?" Darren's thoughts scattered.

"Your girlfriend."

"She's not my—"

Erin gave him a look. "Oh, come on. She just looked at you as if she's wandered the desert and you're fresh water."

Darren felt his face heat. "Yeah, well…"

Erin giggled. "And you looked back the same way."

"Would you stop?"

His little sister grinned. "It's all good. I get it."

Darren didn't like the idea of Erin "getting" anything. His sister might be an adult, but to him, she'd forever be that sweet twelve-year-old who'd begged to tag along.

"What a scowl," Erin teased.

He pinched his sister's knee. "I'm trying to listen."

Erin squirmed, bumping the table. And that earned them a fierce look from their mom.

Darren glanced at Bree.

A hint of a smile hovered around her lips, barely creasing those dimples. She'd seen them alright, but it hadn't thrown off her concentration. This gig was probably child's play for her.

The mini concert ended and the audience clapped. Darren watched as the quartet stood and bowed. Could Bree join them now? The restaurant staff lifted the chafing dish lids on the long buffet table, and folks lined up for brunch. The quartet resumed playing as background music.

He sighed. How long would he have to wait to talk to her?

If he wanted his family to believe he and Bree were merely friends, he'd give her a wave and go. If he was smart, he'd stop seeing her outside the wild edibles class as if they were dating. He'd simply wait until Tuesday to see her again.

If he was smart, he'd stop thinking there could be anything more than merely a brief connection, a temporary courtship with Bree.

Chapter Nine

Darren was early and remained in the van. He wasn't in the mood for today's class. Maybe because Bree's mom planned to go, and that put him under the microscope. Joan Anderson had a way of looking over her glasses at him, as if inspecting and then finding him lacking somehow. It put him on edge.

He'd entered field reports for the last couple of days into his laptop while waiting. The windows were down, but the breeze off the lake was much too warm for early May. Crazy weather. Cold then hot.

"Good, you're here." Stella didn't wait for an invitation. She climbed right up into the front passenger seat.

He hadn't heard her approach and chuckled. "So are you. What's up?"

"I had to drop some letters in the mail, so I left the cottage early. Plus, I'm nosy. What's going on with you and Bree? Joan says you've been spending a lot of time with her."

Darren saved his document and then closed the laptop lid. "Simply showing her the sights as offered at your house over dinner."

Stella gave him a satisfied grin. "Exactly. And?"

"And nothing." But that wasn't true. His attraction to her had started the minute they'd met. No matter how Darren looked at it, this relationship couldn't end well. "It's not like that, Stel. She's a nice girl and all, but—"

Stella narrowed her gaze. "She's no girl. She's a full-grown woman who's accomplished and professional."

All the more reason why she wouldn't stick around. "I realize that, but—"

"But what?"

Darren offered up the easiest excuse handy. "I'm not interested."

Not interested in getting hurt. Not interested in becoming the object of disapproval from yet another Bay Willows family.

"Joan's worried you'll sweep Bree off her feet."

Darren laughed. "Yeah, right."

Stella lowered her voice. "You're the kind of guy Bree needs."

Darren took the bait. "And what kind is that?"

"The kind who will support and cherish her. You're the keeper kind."

Darren snorted. He wouldn't keep well for two years while she chased after whatever it was she wanted. "What makes you think she'd keep me? She just got rid of her last boyfriend."

"Yeah, finally." Stella's expression didn't joke. She looked far too serious.

"What makes you say that?"

"He was very image-oriented. He treated Bree—" Stella suddenly stopped and waved out of the open window.

Bree and her mom pulled into the parking space next to them.

Darren nearly growled. Nice timing. It should have been enough to know that Stella didn't like the way this guy had treated Bree, but it wasn't. Bree had said that her parents had loved the guy.

He got out of the van and spotted crutches in the backseat of Bree's car. As much as he wanted to talk to Bree, he needed to schmooze her mom a little. That meant putting to rest any fears Joan had about him sweeping Bree off her feet. As if he could.

He needed Joan's stamp of approval when it came to job performance. He cleared his throat. "Hi, Joan. Do you need help getting in the van?"

"Thank you, but no, Bree will drive."

He looked at Bree.

"I'll follow you," she said.

Changing the location of today's morel hunt proved a good idea considering Joan's physical limitations. She could hang out on his parents' deck instead of trying to negotiate uneven ground in the woods.

Maybe that would earn him points. His folks were good people. "Let me see your phone."

Bree placed a gold rhinestone–encrusted case in his hand.

He looked at the gaudy thing, flipped it over and then looked at her. "Really?"

"What? Stella gave me that." Her voice challenged him to make something of it.

He chuckled. The case looked like something Stella might pick out. He pulled up Bree's GPS app, punched in his parents' address and then showed her the map. "It's about ten miles north of town, in case we get separated. Watch out for this curve right here." He pointed to the road that suddenly veered left after topping a hill. "It can be dangerous if you're going too fast."

"I'll be careful. Thanks." No irritated tone this time at his caution.

He tapped the roof of her car and looked around.

Across the street he spotted the rest of their class swarming toward them. They looked every bit the country club crowd, dressed in summery shorts and bright colors. Even Ed, who approached from a block away yet, wore a pair of multicolored shorts Darren wouldn't have been caught dead in. As a regional supervisor, Darren would need to lead by example. And that might mean treating the summer crowd a little more softly. Could he do it?

To everything there is a season...

Maybe this was his season of change.

He glanced at Bree still seated in her car, chatting with her mom. The sound of multiple conversations going at once flooded his senses, pushing out his thoughts. He'd been standing around deep in thought while everyone waited for directions. Waited for his leadership. About time he stepped up.

Darren clapped his hands together once. "Let's load up and head out."

In the van, he took a head count and then made his way north to his parents' home. Talk about worlds colliding. He was about to set loose a group of folks from Bay Willows in his family's woods. At least his parents had his back if anything went wrong.

He hoped Bree did, too.

Bree followed Darren as he pulled into a long circular gravel drive surrounded by a rich green lawn. A huge log-styled home that looked like it had been added on to more than once sat farther back. A walkway of flat slabs of stone connected the driveway to a front porch complete with rocking chairs. Talk about country charm.

"This is lovely." Bree's mother gawked out the window.

"Yeah." Bree parked next to the van and peered through the windshield.

This fine home surprised her. Not because of Darren's parents—the place suited them—but considering the chip on their son's shoulder, she would have expected Darren to have grown up somewhere much more modest. The other side of the railroad tracks made more sense than this rolling lakeside retreat.

The passenger side door opened, and Darren offered her mother his hand. "My mom has refreshments on the back deck, and then we'll decide whether to hunt morels or take the tour of the sugar shack first."

"That'd be good." Her mother nodded, clearly impressed.

"I'll get the crutches." Bree dashed around the car in time to see Helen and Andy Zelinsky coming toward them.

"Glad you could make it." Helen reached for Bree's hands. "And I hope you brought your cello."

Bree felt her cheeks warm at the questioning look her mother gave her. "Yes, I did."

"The quartet was fabulous, but I want to hear just you play." Helen looked up. "And ideally that storm will stay away long enough for today's morel hunt."

Bree took in the dark clouds gathering in the western sky. The weather forecast had said nothing about rain today. "Helen, this is my mother and the organizer of the class, Joan Anderson."

"Good to meet you, Joan." Helen glanced at the soft cast and crutches. "I'm sorry, but it's a bit of a hike to the backyard. Maybe we should relocate to the sugar shack."

"Oh, no. I'm fine. Really. The crutches are better support than my cane. At least for now." Her mother had been given the green light to use a cane. She could put weight on her foot, but with caution.

Helen, not looking fully convinced, moved on and greeted the others. She gave Stella a big hug.

"Maybe Darren should carry you," Bree teased.

Her mother glared at her. "I'm perfectly capable of walking."

But Darren had overheard and walked toward them. "Need help?"

Bree had to own that she wouldn't mind being carried by him. "Maybe stand by, in case."

He nodded.

Bree's mother proved them both unneeded as she negotiated the walkway around to the back of the house without incident. The backyard proved even nicer, with frontage on a small inland lake and even a small sandy beach. The deck was expansive, too, with part of it covered. Underneath that generous overhang stood a table laden with iced tea, lemonade and a tray of snacks. Their group surrounded said table without hesitation and gobbled up cheese dip and crackers and homemade cookies.

Darren asked Joan, "Can I get you something to drink?"

"Bree will do that. But thank you."

As Bree waited for an opening around the refreshment table, Stella stood next to her. "Helen's a great cook. I remember Darren once brought me a tray of her homemade pierogi."

"They're nice people." Bree meant it. Darren's parents were real, salt-of-the-earth kind of people. Nothing like Philip's parents, who were stuffy even by her standards.

Philip had been uptight, too, making critical comments about her hair and how she dressed. Even her attempts to help others. She'd given up a midweek gig with a group of struggling young musicians because they'd played in a grungy coffee house in an area Philip hadn't liked.

Bree had been weak then, letting him interfere with her

goals. Seattle promised not only professional dreams but also an escape from the expected routine.

She glanced at Darren. He stood next to his father, and they laughed about something. The affection between the two men was clear. They spoke to each other with mutual respect and acceptance. Darren had found his path. It was no wonder he'd never moved away; he had everything right here.

Bree envied his sense of contentment. She'd feared getting stuck in the same place whereby Darren welcomed it. She wanted change. He didn't. They were two different people chasing completely different things. Not exactly a good foundation for a lasting relationship. They didn't stand a chance.

Thunder rumbled louder. Darren looked up at the sky and frowned. He'd kept his ear tuned into the approaching storm while the group scoured his parents' woods for morels. Whites were popping, and everyone went crazy finding *just one more*.

Lightning flashed. He'd waited too long, and that wasn't smart. Darren blew his whistle. "Let's go. Now."

"It'll blow over." Ed's greedy onion bag bulged with morels.

"I'm not taking any chances." Darren stared the old guy down while the women scurried out of the woods.

He heard Stella shriek when the first gigantic raindrops hit. The window of opportunity to stay dry had definitely closed.

"Fine." Ed moved forward.

"Let's head for the sugar shack. That's closer than the house." Darren brought up the rear with Bree.

"This is kind of fun." She gave him a smile that sliced through him.

Getting caught in the rain with her would have been interesting if they'd been alone. Fortunately, for both their sakes, they weren't. "Yeah, right."

Bree frowned at his sharp tone.

"Look—" The roar of the rain tore at his attempt to apologize. He watched Bree as she ran ahead of him, the rain soaking through her T-shirt and shorts. Let her think he was a grump. That was safer.

The deluge hit while the group was in the middle of his parents' mowed lawn. He'd never seen seventy-year-olds move so fast. When they made it into the sugar shack, his mom met them at the door with a stack of towels.

"Nice touch with these." Darren dried off as he looked around. His mom had brought the party inside the sugar shack. Cozy for sure.

"I heard the thunder, and your father helped me move everything out here. We can hang out comfortably until the weather passes." His mother handed Bree a towel. "I hope you don't mind, but I had Andy bring in your cello case. Your car was unlocked."

"Thank you. Might as well set up now." Bree wrapped the towel around her neck and shoulders, under the fat braid of her hair. Her wet bangs were plastered against her forehead, making her golden eyes seem huge and incredibly pretty.

"Need help?"

"I got it." She waved off his offer.

Darren quickly took a head count. Everyone accounted for. No one lost but him. Every time he looked at Bree.

His mom had everything in hand like always. She'd make this his best class yet with such a party atmosphere. Laughter rang through their gathering as his class attendees dried off. The stainless steel evaporator gleamed, reflecting their little group crammed into this small space.

Folding chairs had been set up for seating in addition to the benches against the wall.

Funny, but Darren didn't feel crowded.

Stella and Ed and the rest helped themselves to the snacks his mom had set out on the huge oak desk. He and Matthew had moved that desk out of Annie's house last year. When he'd been afraid to walk around in his own hometown. That time seemed far away.

He watched Bree push a folding chair into a corner near the light of a window. Carefully she opened her case, pulled out the gleaming wooden cello and settled it against her leg while she grabbed her bow. Even in a damp T-shirt and shorts, Bree looked refined.

"She's good for you," his mom whispered as she wrapped her arm around his waist. "She brings you back to life."

"She's leaving for two years." It came out a low growl.

His mom rubbed his back, slow and comforting like when he was little. "I'm sorry, honey."

He shrugged off her touch. "It's no big deal."

Rain clanged against the tin roof above. Lightning flashed, followed by a clap of thunder so loud that it rattled the windows. A couple of the women squealed, then laughed.

Darren hoped that wasn't an answer to his fib. Bree was turning into a very big deal. He watched her as those first mellow notes she played seeped into space, quieting the chatter. He didn't recognize the tune; he wouldn't. He didn't listen to this kind of stuff. Maybe he should. The silky sound of whatever it was she played captivated him. Her cello coupled with the rhythmic beats of rain hitting the roof mesmerized all of them into silence.

Bree gave him a soft smile, making her dimples a whisper. He smiled back. His mom said she was good for him.

Maybe that was true. She'd drawn him out of the gloom he'd been under for a long while.

Bree focused on playing.

Darren didn't look away. He watched her fingers slide up and down the neck of the instrument with confidence. She tilted the bow with such grace, nodding her head in time with the music.

"She's good," his mom whispered.

He nodded. "Too good for here."

Bree played piece after piece as the storm rumbled away into the distance, leaving behind a soft rain. Occasionally she'd look into Darren's intense gaze. His bright blue eyes burned through her, shooting sparks to her fingers and toes. She played to him.

It had quieted down enough to hear about the maple operation and had been for a few minutes now. She finished the piece and leaned back, feeling oddly drained.

"Aww." One of the women said. "Don't stop."

"It's close to end time." Bree looked at Darren for help, but he didn't seem in any hurry to leave.

"One more." Darren's voice coaxed, impossible to refuse.

"Yes, encore. Encore," some of the others chanted.

"Okay. Here's one that I composed, but it's not finished yet." Bree launched into the restless piece she'd been working on since applying for the music residency.

She'd added to it after coming up north. She'd added more after meeting Darren, but the remainder of the piece eluded her. Like the future path she'd committed to taking, the music twisted and turned only to stop, waiting for the next chord. The next step in her life.

She held her bow still and took a deep breath to calm her racing pulse. "That's it."

Stella clapped first. Followed by the rest of the class.

Bree glanced at Darren.

He gave her a quick nod.

What was he thinking? Any thoughts about her? Lately, he'd taken center stage in her mind.

Bree blew out her breath, stood and bowed. "Thanks. I'll turn it over to our hosts."

Helen Zelinsky spoke up. "Thank you so much for playing, Bree. It was beautiful. If everyone will gather round, Andy will explain how we turn sap into syrup, and then we have a little something for you to take home."

Bree quietly returned her cello to its case while listening to Darren's father. The process of collecting sap, boiling it down to syrup and then bottling it sounded like hard work. It had to be. Creating something so sweet didn't just happen.

She glanced at Darren again. Something sweet boiled between them, too, but it wouldn't keep. How could it from such a distance away? Literally across the country.

She heard Ed peppering Andy Zelinsky with questions.

Darren made his way toward her and pointed his thumb at the group. "I guess I'm not the only one he challenges."

Bree whispered back, "Maybe it's a compliment, him giving you a hard time."

"Maybe." He reached for her cello case. "I'll load this in your car."

"I've got it." Bree stalled him. She didn't let people carry her case. His parents had grabbed it earlier without any damage, but she hadn't known about it.

He lifted his hands in surrender, smiling. "Okay."

She tried to listen to the presentation, but her focus was shot with Darren standing so close.

"That was amazing, by the way," he whispered near her ear.

"Yeah?" Bree reeled, feeling the warmth of his breath brush her skin. Darren's father still spoke in the background, wrapping up his speech. Class was over but Bree wished it wasn't. She wished—

"So, what inspired you to write that last song?"

"A lot of things." Bree lifted her cello case, putting space between them.

"Anything from up here?"

Should she tell him that he'd been part of what she'd composed? Her feelings for Darren had translated well into notes on a page. Really well. "Some."

He gave her a languid smile. "Tell me."

The pull between them tightened.

Andy Zelinsky walked past them with a box. The entire class swelled around him as he handed out small bottles of maple syrup.

Bree stepped back to get out of the way and bumped into Darren. She froze when his hand slipped to her waist in an attempt to guide her forward. She closed her eyes. Only for a second to savor the rush of his touch before moving away. "Thanks."

"No problem." His voice sounded rough.

Bree focused on making it out the door, bulky cello case in hand. At the door, she set down her instrument and reached for Helen's hands. "Thank you for making this class special."

Helen pulled her into a hug instead. "You made the day. God's got plans for you, my dear. Stay tuned into that."

Bree returned the embrace, careful not to hang on too tightly. How'd this woman know she searched for her place in the world? How much more could she see?

Bree pulled back but didn't meet Helen's gaze. "Thank you."

Darren's mom smiled. "You're welcome."

Bree quickly made her escape. Outside the rain had stopped, leaving behind clear skies and sweet-smelling air. The Zelinskys' lawn glittered like diamonds where sunshine hit water droplets clinging for life. Another half hour or so and the grass would be dry. The sparkle faded like a memory.

Bree glanced at her left hand, which was bare of any rings. She wore no jewelry but a watch around her wrist that showed they'd gone over their class time yet again.

She glanced at her mother hobbling ahead on crutches. Would she mind that they'd gone long? Bree's heart pinched at the thought of leaving, of moving so far away.

"Beautiful playing, Bree." Stella grinned at her as they approached the driveway. "It sounded different than when you practice."

Bree tipped her head. "What do you mean?"

"More passionate." Stella winked.

Bree's stomach flipped. "Oh, well, I, uh—"

"It's okay, honey. That's a good thing. Don't ever be afraid to feel."

Surely Stella didn't see into her heart, too. "Thanks. I'll remember that."

"See that you do."

Bree lifted the hatchback of her car, settled her cello inside and closed the trunk with a soft clunk. She spotted Darren on his cell phone, his brow knitted together and his face ashen.

Bree's stomach tightened. She was feeling—feeling like something was terribly wrong. She strained to listen, but the chatter of Stella and Ed and the others as they loaded into the van kept her from hearing anything clearly.

When she overheard Darren mention the hospital, she moved toward him and touched his arm. After he pocketed his phone, she asked, "What is it?"

Darren's parents stood close enough to hear, too, and both looked worried.

"That was Kate. Neil's been in a motorcycle accident. They're at the hospital and it doesn't look good."

Bree squeezed his forearm. "I'll take you there."

Darren looked like he'd been whipped. "But the van."

Andy Zelinsky stepped in. "Give me the keys. I'll drive them back."

"But—"

Helen backed him up. "I'll drive Joan and then bring your dad home. Darren, go with Bree."

Bree felt thrown into a bad dream. She'd spent enough time with Kate and Neil over the weekend to care. They'd been nice to her. And now? She closed her eyes.

Dear Lord, please touch Neil and be with Kate.

Darren handed over the keys to his father and then reached toward her for hers. "Let's go."

"I'll drive. Get in." Bree turned to her mother. "I'm not sure when I'll be home. Will you be okay?"

"Of course. Go." Her mother glanced at Darren, then back to her. "And be careful."

Bree didn't waste more time. Darren had slid into the passenger seat. He looked like he expected to lose his friend.

Please, God. Not more loss for him. Not this way.

Bree slid behind the wheel and clicked her seat belt. She noticed that Darren hadn't. "Buckle up."

He complied but didn't say a word.

Pulling out of the Zelinskys' driveway, she drove back the way they'd come. She needed to get him there fast but in one piece; she let up some from the gas pedal. "What happened?"

He shrugged. "Kate said he'd hit a deer."

"Oh." Bad news.

"It was raining."

Worse news. "I'm so sorry."

"Just drive." Darren's voice was low and craggy-sounding. The man was scared.

Bree covered his hand and squeezed. Her breath caught when Darren threaded his fingers through hers and tightened his hold. She prayed again. The same prayer as before.

This wasn't good. Not good at all.

Chapter Ten

No one liked hospitals, with the antiseptic smells and winding hallways that required instructions to find a room. Darren was no exception. He wiped the palms of his hands on his pants before entering the emergency room.

The TV blared in the main waiting area, where several people sat. He didn't see Kate. Had they moved Neil to a room already? Maybe everything was okay. He stepped up to the nurses' station and gave his friend's name.

"Oh. The family are gathered in the small waiting room around the corner." Her face looked grave. Much too grave.

That look hit him in the midsection, stealing away his breath. Neil was hurt badly and there was nothing Darren could do to change that. One more thing he couldn't control.

He felt Bree's hand slip into his own.

For a moment, he'd forgotten she'd come with him. His throat closed up tight as he squeezed her hand, grateful for her calming presence.

They turned a corner and entered the smaller waiting room. Kate looked up, her eyes puffy and red. Neil's parents were there, too. Darren opened his mouth to speak, but nothing came out.

"Any news?" Bree rushed toward Kate, hands out-stretched.

Darren watched his friend's wife hold on to Bree as if she were a lifeline. *What if Neil*— He didn't finish his thought. He couldn't. Darren had known Neil most of his life. He was a nice guy who didn't deserve this freak ac-cident.

"We're waiting to hear." Kate reached toward him.

He grabbed her hand and squeezed. He still couldn't seem to form the right words, but Kate understood. She gave him a watery smile.

More people entered the waiting room—the minister who'd married Kate and Neil, followed by Kate's parents. Kate leaned against her mom while the minister offered to pray. More hand-holding.

Bree stood beside him and grabbed his hand.

Darren couldn't focus on the minister's words. All he could think of was what Neil faced. Would he come out of this the same? What if he didn't? What then?

"Amen," Bree whispered, but didn't let go.

They sat down and waited. Darren listened to Kate ex-plain what had happened in a soft, broken voice.

Her mother cried.

After fifteen minutes, Darren couldn't take the hushed voices, the tears. He stood and stared a moment at the cof-fee dispenser on a counter near a small sink, along with cups, sugar and powdered creamer. Bad coffee was not what he needed.

"I'm going for something to drink. Can I get anyone anything?"

Folks shook their heads.

"I'll go with you." Bree followed him out.

Darren walked the hallway, took a couple of turns and stopped where it dead-ended at an open area with a couch.

A wall of windows showcased a spectacular view of Maple Bay. He glanced at the small table beside the couch. It held an open Bible and a lamp that had been left on.

The urge to clear off that table with one swipe overwhelmed him, so he stepped closer to the window and bumped his forehead against the cool glass, helpless.

Bree didn't say a word, but stood close. Right next to him, offering her support if he needed it.

He needed far more.

Darren touched her fat braid. Feeling its weight, he lifted it and pulled off the elastic band at the end. Then he unraveled the strands, threading his fingers through the mink-colored mass of hair. It felt silky-soft and pretty. Like her. He let her hair drop against her shoulder.

Bree searched his eyes. "What can I do?"

Make things stay the same.

He'd almost said it aloud. Bree couldn't turn back the clock any more than she could change her plans to leave. Her future promised a different path than his. A path far away. He handed back the elastic band.

Bree took it without a word and then wrapped her arms around his waist. She rested her head against his shoulder.

Darren didn't dare move. He kept his arms at his sides, draped over hers, and closed his eyes fighting his desire to touch her. Whatever was between them couldn't end well, and holding her was only going to make things worse.

When Bree drew away, he reacted and pulled her back, only closer. He buried his face in her neck, into all that hair he'd let loose. She smelled good, like flowers and sunshine and rain.

She trembled.

Maybe that shudder had come from him.

"Darren?" Her whisper should have warned him to back away, but it sounded more like a question. Or a plea.

Darren answered the only way he knew how. Crushing his lips against hers, he kissed her.

A few minutes later, Bree stared at Darren's broad shoulders. She'd pulled her hair back, anchoring it at the base of her neck with the elastic band Darren had pulled out of her hair.

Now was not the time to fall in love.

Certainly not in such a short time, but then, feelings this strong and reckless were new to her. Scary, too. She followed him back to the waiting room with an unopened soft drink can in her hand that made her fingers cold.

They'd shared only a couple of kisses. Kisses of comfort that she'd hoped to ease his worry. Her hopes had backfired the moment she deepened the kiss. Backfired, big-time. Who'd she think she was kidding? She'd wanted to kiss him. Wanted him to kiss her back and keep kissing her. But Darren had soon skittered away from her like a spooked rabbit. He wouldn't look her in the eyes when he'd mumbled that they should return.

Bree walked behind him, boring holes into his back with no success of seeing into his heart. They entered the small waiting room filled with new tension. Everyone looked ready to burst into tears, and guilt immediately smote her for worrying over a kiss.

She watched as a doctor talked to Kate. He spoke too low for Bree to hear, but from the look on Kate's face, the news wasn't good. Bree glanced at Darren.

He ran a hand through his hair. He must have been able to hear the news, because his eyes grew shiny wet as whatever the doctor shared with Kate sunk in.

Bree wanted to go to him but stayed put. Now wasn't the time for embraces, nor could she share her feelings. Bree needed to leave him alone.

The doctor left and people swarmed Kate.

Darren leaned close and whispered near Bree's ear. "You might as well go home. I'll catch a ride back to Bay Willows later for the van. It looks like a rough night ahead."

Staying wouldn't be good for either of them; she might do something else she'd regret. "How bad?"

"Neil's in surgery. They're hoping to save his leg, but there's a lot of damage."

Bree cupped her mouth.

Darren awkwardly patted her back. "Go on. Go home."

She nodded and slipped out of the room unnoticed. Heart heavy, Bree made her way out to her car. Climbing behind the wheel, she placed the can of pop into the cup holder and rested her forehead on the steering wheel. Tears ran down her face, so Bree gave in and cried.

Her phone rang.

"Hello?"

"Bree? Baby, what's wrong?"

Philip!

Her stomach turned and she sniffed. Why hadn't she checked who it was? Or let it go to voice mail? "It's nothing."

"Sounds like something."

She cleared her throat, hating the edge in Philip's voice that wasn't concern. "A friend's in the hospital."

"What friend?"

"You don't know him." Bree sniffed again.

Silence.

"Was there a reason you called?"

"Yes, actually there was." Philip chuckled. An irritating sound. "I was thinking about coming up. Take in some golf and give you a good send-off."

Bree closed her eyes. "Please don't."

"There's no reason we can't be friendly, Bree. Our parents are friends."

There was every reason. "Philip, please."

"Think about it." He paused and then added, "Sorry about your friend."

"Thanks."

He disconnected.

Bree stared at her phone. Why wouldn't he leave her alone?

She drove toward Bay Willows, but instead of pulling into her parents' driveway, she headed for Stella's cottage. She passed by the community building where Darren's work van sat parked. Seeing that green vehicle brought new tears to her eyes.

At Stella's, Bree got out, bounded up the porch stairs and knocked.

Stella opened the door wide. "Bree, come in. You okay?"

"I don't think so." She walked into her friend's open arms.

Stella gathered her close and led her toward the kitchen. "Tell me what happened. Is his friend going to be okay?"

"They're not sure." Bree explained the situation while Stella made tea.

"That's not what's really bothering you, though, is it?" Her elderly friend set a cup of herbal tea on the table along with the honeypot.

Bree shook her head. "I have feelings for Darren."

Stella brushed aside Bree's bangs like she was a child with a skinned knee. "Is that such a bad thing?"

"It's the last thing either of us wants."

"Why?"

"Because I'm leaving in two weeks. I'm not passing up my chance to do something special, and I'm not getting stuck here."

Stella frowned. "How do you know there's nothing here for you?"

"I just know." After talking to Jan Nelson, the Bay Willows music school looked unlikely to get off the ground anytime soon. The board couldn't agree on who they wanted to reach or what venue they'd provide. There were few opportunities here for her.

Bree sipped her tea, but it didn't quell her concerns, her fear.

"Has Darren asked you to stay?"

"No." He might not return her feelings. Even after that earth-shaking kiss. She grabbed the little ceramic pot decorated with bees and drizzled more honey into her tea.

"Then there's nothing to worry about. Right?" Stella's expression betrayed that sentiment. She looked concerned too.

"You're probably right." Bree joined Stella in putting up a good front, but it didn't make her feel any better.

She wanted more with Darren, but it'd be a huge mistake to give up this opportunity. One she'd regret the rest of her days. That kind of resentment wouldn't be fair to him. She'd resent staying behind to see where this went, and then what if they ended up nowhere?

Her plans had been so clear before. Why so much muddiness after a kiss? Didn't seem fair having to choose between following her dreams and her heart.

"I think I should leave early for Seattle." Bree could run, away from her feelings and the man who owned them.

"When?"

Her mother wasn't quite ready to take over the class, but she would be after next week. Bree would simply steer clear of Darren until then. No more off-the-beaten-path outings. And no more kisses. Vacation was officially over. She'd miss Memorial Day with her family if she left early, but the Anderson barbecue and the Maple Springs parade were small sacrifices in the scheme of things. Her heart twisted. Some things couldn't be helped.

"After the next class."

Stella gave her a sad-eyed look of disappointment. "Falling in love is not the end of the world."

"For me, it is." Bree ran her finger around the rim of the tea cup. "For me, it sure is."

Darren's phone whistled with an incoming text. He waited until he stopped his truck at a red light before checking who it came from.

Bree.

How's Neil?

Guilt ripped through him. He should have called her or texted. He should have let her know last night when things had improved, but he'd been spent. He called her.

"Hey, Darren." Her voice sounded incredibly soft.

Remembering the feel of her hair and the texture of her lips, he gritted his teeth. "Neil is stable. Are you home?"

"Yes, but—"

"Can I swing by?"

"Umm. Sure."

"See you in about ten minutes."

He'd planned on seeing Bree today anyway. He would have called her from the hospital, maybe to meet up for dinner or something. They needed to have a talk. He blew out his breath. He couldn't use Neil's accident as an excuse for the way he'd kissed her. It'd be convenient—understandable, even—but false. He'd kissed her because he'd wanted to. Plain and simple.

Only it didn't feel simple. That couple of kisses hadn't

been enough. He wanted more than she could give him. More than he should ask for.

When he pulled up in front of the Anderson cottage, Bree was there, waiting for him on the porch. Her hair hung loose, draping her shoulders, but worry marred her pretty brow.

She hurried toward him, scanning his faded jeans and cotton shirt. "No work today?"

"I took the day off."

"Can we walk?" Bree scrunched her nose. That meant she needed to talk, too. More scary stuff.

He surveyed the neighboring cottages. More of them were opening up now, getting ready for summer. Gardeners worked on lawns or planted flower beds and boxes. Raleigh's family usually arrived after Memorial Day, so she wouldn't be around Bay Willows when the hired help was opening up the cottage. He'd always had a better chance of running into her in town anyway.

No matter how he sliced it, he was a baby. Scared of the woman he used to love and scared of the woman he could love if she stuck around.

"How about down by the water?" he suggested.

"I know a shortcut. Come on." Bree waved him out of the truck. "You said Neil is stable. What's that mean?"

Darren ran a hand through his hair and got out of his truck. "I'm sorry I didn't text you or call last night. The surgeon saved his leg. They pumped him full of antibiotics and he responded well. The doctors expect a good recovery in time. He woke up after surgery, and Kate was able to talk to him."

"Thank You, God." Bree closed her eyes. Her concern was real. She truly cared.

Guilt smacked him again. He hadn't given her enough credit. He'd lumped her in with what he'd thought were pretentious summer folk. People he'd resented since he was a kid. He'd even kept the comparison of her to his ex-fiancée alive after it was obvious that Bree wasn't anything like Raleigh. Bree was different. Special.

"I was on my way to see him when you texted."

Her brow furrowed again, and she stopped walking. "Oh, I'm sorry. Did you need to go?"

He shook his head. "I'll go later. I needed to see you today. To talk."

"Yes. Me, too." Bree slipped through a hedge of bushes on a worn downhill path to the lake. "Watch your step."

The incline was indeed steep, but short. Lazy waves lapped against the sand mixed with rocks and pebbles. Many docks had been installed for the season and reached out like fingers into Maple Bay.

They crossed the road onto a narrow sidewalk that followed the shoreline. The warm sun caressed his back and shoulders until the lakeside breeze blew in crisp over the still chilly waters.

Bree shivered and crossed her arms.

Darren wrapped his arm around her, drawing her close. "Cold?"

She tensed but didn't pull away. "Thanks."

He might as well start the conversation they needed to have. "I'm not sorry I kissed you."

"I am."

He stopped and faced her. "Why?"

She wouldn't look at him. Her gaze hit him somewhere in the middle of his chest.

He lifted her chin and ran his fingertip where her dimples showed when she smiled. Bree wasn't smiling now. "Why are you sorry?"

She glared at him. "Because I have feelings for you. Because I'm leaving soon and I don't want to—"

He leaned down and kissed her. Quick and hard.

She pushed him away. "That's not helping."

Hearing her admit that she cared did something to him. Something he didn't expect. Something he didn't want to lose. "Why Seattle? Do you really have to go way out there?"

"Seriously? Don't even think of asking me to stay." Now she looked angry.

He didn't want to let this die, but then, what kind of chance did they have after only a few dates? "I suppose we can keep in touch."

That sounded lame even to his ears. They'd known each other only a couple of weeks, but that was long enough to have *feelings* for each other. Very real feelings he should have known better than to pursue. Hadn't he learned his lesson? Whirlwind romances didn't last.

Even if they kept in touch, he knew how it'd go. They'd do fine for the first few months, until the novelty wore off. They couldn't maintain a long-distance relationship for two years. When Bree left, they'd be done. He'd known that all along and yet he'd let her in. He'd let himself care.

"I suppose we could." She bit her bottom lip. She wasn't convinced, either.

He wanted to kiss her again but started walking instead. "It is what it is."

"Right," she agreed, skipping to catch up. "What happened last night is reason enough not to get involved, considering the circumstances. We can remain friends."

Darren let loose a sarcastic chuckle. There was no going back to that, not after that kiss. They might have something to build on if distance wasn't an issue, but— He looked up and froze.

Heart pounding in his ears, Darren stared at his ex-fiancée, hand in hand with Tony, walking the shoreline. The couple was headed straight for them.

Bree saw them, too.

He stared at Raleigh's cool gaze and didn't look away. The woman seemed perfectly at ease, as if it was no big deal what she'd done to him.

He curled his hands into fists but forced them back open when he felt Bree's touch to his arm. He took a deep breath. He'd been running from this moment for over a year and a half. Today he faced his past. Ironic, considering he discussed his future with Bree.

He didn't move or speak. He simply stood there and stared at the two of them. At least Tony looked uncomfortable, and that gave Darren some satisfaction.

"Hi, Darren." Raleigh stopped in front of him. Her blond hair glimmered in the sunshine, but she didn't look as good as he remembered. She looked thinner. More hollow. Her heavily made up eyes narrowed. "And Bree. I didn't know you two knew each other."

"Yeah." Darren didn't offer any explanations.

"How are you?" Bree's voice lacked its usual warmth. If he hadn't known her, he wouldn't have been able to tell she was being short. Almost rude—for her.

"Can't complain." Raleigh flicked her hair over her shoulder.

That was a new one. He seemed to remember that Raleigh typically had something to complain about. Darren looked at his friend, the guy he'd grown up with. They'd ridden the bus together, played sports and pretty much shared everything. He could add girlfriends to that list now.

Darren curled his fists again. "Tony."

Tony finally met his gaze. He looked sheepish, as if thinking the same thing as Darren. "How've you been?"

That was the question of the century. Being chased out of his own hometown for fear of this face-to-face pretty much summed up how he'd been. No matter how much he wanted to vent, Darren didn't bother. The effort didn't seem worth it anymore. "I've had my moments."

That got to Raleigh. She kicked at an imaginary pebble on the sidewalk. "We're moving to St. Louis at the end of the month. Tony accepted a position there. Good future and all."

Darren clenched his jaw. They both chased a lifestyle instead of a life. He expected to feel angry, but the sadness that shot through his veins surprised him. There was no going back for them. Things had changed forever.

Darren was suddenly okay with that. Finally. "I hope you guys find what you're looking for."

Raleigh's eyes widened at the resignation in his voice. She looked unsettled as if his forgiveness wasn't something she expected. He might have misread her. He'd been good at misreading her. "Yeah, you too."

Darren stepped off the sidewalk to let them pass. He didn't look back. He felt Bree's hand slip into his own and gave her fingers a squeeze. "Want to grab lunch?"

Bree looked back at the man and woman who'd once torn his world apart. "Are you okay?"

Darren considered the question. Was he? "Doesn't matter."

"Do you want to talk about it?"

"No. I'm done with all that. With them." Glancing at Bree's hand wrapped firmly in his own made him wonder if maybe he'd found what he truly wanted.

Bree was real and she cared. Problem was, he didn't want her to leave. But by asking her to stay, he might lose her forever.

Chapter Eleven

Darren's stony expression made Bree nervous. He was either angry or hurting or both and she didn't know how to help. So she remained silent as they cut through the line of willow trees that marked the main entrance of Bay Willows.

The sidewalk ended but they continued walking, through the public boat launch toward the public beach. The sun shone high in the sky, making the blue waters of Maple Bay glimmer. A couple of sailboats skimmed the horizon.

She should say something.

"Want to sit down?" Darren broke their silence and headed for one of several park benches. "I don't really want lunch, do you?"

Bree scrunched her nose. She'd eaten breakfast a couple of hours before Darren had picked her up. She slipped next to him but not too close. "No. Not really. I'm sorry about running into them."

Darren shrugged. "Bound to happen. I don't know what I was so worried about."

"Maybe you weren't ready before." Bree took in the view and sighed. "Beautiful, isn't it?"

"I think so." Darren gazed out at the lake a moment and then turned toward her. "Why isn't this enough for you people?"

You people? Bree didn't react to the harsh tone of his voice. "What do you mean?"

He leaned his elbows on his knees. The blue polo shirt he wore stretched taut across his back, begging for her touch. She kept her hands to herself. He didn't look like he'd welcome her comfort.

He sat back and blew out his breath. "All my life I've heard summer residents say they could never live up here year-round. It's too small, there isn't a mall, there isn't this or that. They complain about all the things that make Maple Springs special, yet every summer, here you all come."

Bree shifted. "For many, it's an escape up north. A good vacation place that's just not reality."

He gave her a hard look. "What about you?"

She stared straight back. Bree didn't like where this was going. "I love a good vacation like everyone else, and thanks to you, that's exactly what I had."

"So that's it. That's all this has been. Just forget about your feelings?"

Feelings she'd admitted to not wanting. "I have to."

"Why?"

Her defenses rose. "If I wasn't satisfied playing with the symphony in Detroit, a small regional chamber orchestra up here won't fill the gap. It can't provide the opportunities I need."

He leaned back, making the park bench squeak. "Be careful chasing ideals and bright lights. Sometimes the simple things are what matter most in life. And sometimes, the most fulfilling."

She didn't want to hear it, especially from him. Who

was he angry with? Raleigh or her? Maybe both. "Why the big chip on your shoulder when it comes to the resort crowd? And why on earth would you fall for someone like Raleigh?"

His blue eyes glittered with anger.

Bree might have pushed him too far, but instead of trying to smooth it over or backtrack, she remained quiet. Waiting. She wanted to know.

Finally, he said, "See that raft over there in the swimming area?"

Bree nodded.

"Growing up, winter was tough for me as a kid. We lived far out and there was little to do after school before we got into high school sports. Come spring, my brothers and I stayed in town after school. We'd hang out and we owned this beach. At least until the summer crowd showed up and we had to share. I didn't like sharing."

Bree could easily picture Darren as the kid he'd painted. Roaming around this small town with an arrogance of his own. "And?"

He shrugged. "As far as I was concerned, that raft belonged to me and mine as soon as the water warmed enough to get in it. We'd earned it after the boredom of a long winter. And no one tested us, no one tried to take it from us, until summer break and the Bay Willows crowd came. You guys have your own private beach barred to locals, but every year your kids had to have our beach and raft. One summer, I'd had enough and took a stand. My brothers and cousins had my back."

"How old were you?"

He shrugged. "Maybe thirteen."

"What happened?"

"A fight ensued, and Parks and Recreation posted two lifeguards at the public beach from then on. One on the raft and one near the bathhouse. It might sound silly now, but I got the message loud and clear. The summer crowd comes first. As a kid I didn't understand how much this town relied on the dollars tourists bring to the area. I felt diminished, as if locals get the scraps. I was sick of coming in second place."

"You've been protecting your town ever since, trying to hang on to what's yours."

"Something like that." He stared out over the bay.

It made sense. And must have made Raleigh's betrayal slice even deeper. Darren was stuck in old resentments, and she didn't want to get stuck.

He looked at her, and something shifted between them. A new level of understanding. "I've got to head back. Are you walking with me?"

"Yes, I'll walk with you." She stood.

He hadn't invited her to visit Neil, but then, she didn't expect him to. She had her cello practice yet to do. Still, she didn't like things left between them like this. An uncomfortable impasse. She held out her hand. "Friends?"

He took her hand and squeezed before letting go. "Always."

Did he mean it? She hoped so. She didn't have much time for close friends but knew Darren could be one of them. He could be more if she wasn't leaving. Much more.

As they walked back the way they'd come, Bree prayed this music residency would finally answer her own needs to be more. Chasing shadows of something she couldn't even name was getting old, but she couldn't give up on her dreams of composing yet. Not without hearing her music played. Not without making some kind of impact.

Bree glanced at Darren. Hands in pockets, he looked pretty gloomy. "Tell me about foraging for asparagus in the next class," she said. "It's one of my favorite vegetables."

He chuckled. "You're in for a treat. I've been out to a couple of spots and cut the ferns so we'll have lots of good shoots to pick for class."

"How will you remember where they are? The ones you cut." They rounded the corner, and her parents' cottage came into view. Too soon, their walk was over, but at least it ended on a lighter note, talking about class. She walked him to his truck.

"I'll remember."

She had no doubt that would be true. Stella had once said that Darren knew the woods and countryside like the back of his hand. Like he owned it. In a way, he did. This area was his home, a place he loved the way she loved music. That'd never change.

She smiled up at him. "Thank you for stopping by. And for our talk."

He looked like he wanted to say more.

Bree was glad he didn't. Her mind was set on leaving, but it wasn't as if she didn't have her doubts.

"See you Tuesday." He slid into the driver's seat.

Her heart broke at the finality in his voice. No more off-the-beaten-path trips or spending time alone. Not if she wanted to stay committed to leaving.

"See you Tuesday." She waved as he pulled out.

She'd say goodbye after class and hope Darren made good on keeping in touch. For now, that's about all she could do.

When Tuesday's class came, Bree was a bundle of conflicting emotions. She could hardly wait to get settled in and explore the artsy neighborhood of her residency in Seattle. She'd checked the area out online. It looked so different from where she'd lived and worked in Midtown

Detroit. Half the country away, but she looked forward to scouring the eclectic shops and downtown center.

Darren hadn't texted her, but then, she'd always been the one to text first. She didn't have much to say, and that didn't bode well for staying in touch after she left. After saying goodbye tonight.

She finished lacing up her trail boots and glanced at her phone again. No texts. Not one. Not even from Philip, which was a welcome relief. She slipped the phone in the back pocket of her jeans and found a restaurant receipt from her lunch with Kate a couple of days ago. Staring at it, Bree sighed. She crumpled it up and threw it in the trash before heading downstairs.

Bree had sent a plant to Neil and Kate at the hospital. She'd made sure to include a get-well card with her cell phone number in case they needed anything. Kate had called right away to thank her, and they'd met for lunch. Neil was doing well, and Bree had admitted to caring for Darren.

Kate hadn't been surprised. She'd encouraged her to go through with her plans, though, stating that if what they'd started was real, they'd make it last. Easy for her to say. Kate spoke from a different place, though. Her husband could have been killed in that motorcycle accident. Time could be cut short when least expected. All the more reason not to leave anything undone or unsaid.

Bree met her mom in the kitchen. "Are you ready?"

"You go ahead. I think I'll drive so I don't have to climb into that van with a cane."

"I can take you." Her mother drove a sporty little crossover SUV that would do fine on the dirt roads they'd likely take, but Bree didn't want her mom getting lost.

Her mother looked away. "You go on ahead to the community building. I'll be there shortly and then we'll see."

Bree hesitated. "You're sure? I can wait."

Her mother waved her away, agitated. "Go. I'll see you in a bit."

"Okay." Bree grabbed her edibles basket and headed out the door.

Another glorious day greeted her, along with newly arrived neighbors waving their hellos. Bay Willows had sprung to life with Memorial Day weekend only a few days away. Traffic had picked up, too, as the summer crowd descended. The image of Darren as a boy defending that raft at the beach flashed through her mind. His place would always be here.

She quickly walked the couple of blocks to the community building. Sure enough, Darren's van sat parked in front. Her pulse raced even as her pace slowed. Five days. She hadn't seen or heard from him in five days. She'd better get used to missing him. Plain and simple.

Darren stepped out of the building and spotted her. "Hello."

"Hi." She fought the urge to throw herself into his arms. "Need help with anything?"

"Nothing to do, really, but wait. Did you bring a knife?"

Bree tipped her head back and groaned. "No. I forgot."

He smiled. "I've got extras for those of you who don't check your calendar list."

"Good." She couldn't think of anything else to say, so she stood next to him, waiting quietly for everyone else to arrive.

Darren was quiet, too.

They'd been reduced to inane small talk—as if nothing had happened between them. No kisses, no baring of their souls. Bree had thanked Darren for a good vacation. They'd had many moments that she'd cherish as memories, but like all vacations, they came to an end. Their relationship would too.

"Great day today." Ed walked toward them and patted his side. He wore a leather sheath attached to his belt. "Got my knife."

"Nice." That was no knife. More like a small machete. Bree giggled and glanced at Darren.

He smiled, as well.

Bree was going to miss this class and the comradery she'd had with the group.

Be careful chasing ideals and bright lights. Sometimes the simple things are what matter most in life.

Darren's words echoed through her mind, taunting her. She'd miss him. Maybe more than she expected.

"Beautiful day, isn't it?" Stella walked toward their little group and gave Bree's back a comforting touch. "How are you?"

Bree's eyes burned. Clearing her throat, she forced a bright smile. "Ready to find wild asparagus."

"Me, too." Stella's concerned gaze didn't miss a thing. "I'm here if you need me."

Bree looked away. "I know. Thanks."

"Let's load up." Darren opened the van doors. Once everyone had climbed inside, he took a quick head count like always.

"Can we wait a couple more minutes for my mother?" Bree pulled out her phone, ready to call her, when a bright blue Cadillac coupe pulled in next to them and honked.

Bree knew that car.

Her mother sat in the passenger seat and opened the window. "We'll follow the van."

Bree stared, her stomach turning.

"Hi, Bree." Philip's voice sounded smooth as satin and equally slippery.

She glared at her mother. Her mother's bit about driving separately was a ruse. She'd known Philip was coming up north. After she'd asked him not to, Philip had persuaded her mother to give him an invitation.

"He wanted to surprise you." Her mother gave her a sheepish smile as if that made everything okay.

Philip smiled. "Surprised?"

"Not really." Bree climbed into the van and stared straight ahead.

She heard her mother's gasp. "Bree…"

Darren approached the Cadillac. "It's a ways out where we are headed." He jotted something down on a piece of paper in his tidy little notebook and handed it to her mother. "If we get separated, we'll meet up at this general store. That's the address and my cell number."

"Okay." Her mother nodded.

Bree peeked into the Cadillac, catching Philip giving Darren a once-over. Something about the hard line of Philip's mouth made her want to spit nails. He had no right to be jealous. No right to be here.

Darren climbed into the driver's seat. "Everyone buckled in and ready?"

Their group chorused agreement.

He looked at her. "Bree?"

"Yes?"

"Your seat belt."

She fumbled with her phone and dropped it. She started to pick it up, but Darren got there first.

He handed it back and touched her hand. "I take it that's *your* ex."

She nodded.

"You okay?"

She grabbed her seat belt and buckled up. "Yes. I'm fine."

Darren watched her closely.

She looked away. "Let's just go."

So that was the guy. Philip. Bree's ex-boyfriend. Darren glanced in the van's rearview mirror. The flashy blue coupe followed close behind. He'd gotten a good look at him before they'd left Bay Willows and Darren didn't like what he saw. Philip dripped success with his styled blond hair and straight white teeth. There wasn't the air of wannabe successful ambition that Tony had. This guy was already there.

If Bree had broken up with a guy like Philip to pursue her dreams of composing, what chance did Darren have?

None.

He pulled onto a dirt road that led to the first foraging spot. Dust flew and Darren couldn't deny the pleasure in knowing that Philip's expensive car was getting dirty. Nice and dirty.

Cresting a small hill, Darren pulled over. This was a desolate spot save for the large farm in the distance. All along the roadside and up against old barbed wire fencing grew the wild asparagus.

Last week, Darren had cut down most of the old fern stalks, but he'd left a few to mark where he'd been. He could see from here where new sprouts had grown up tall. These would be easy pickings for everyone.

He turned in his seat. "You guys know the drill. Meet me at the back of the van for instructions and whistles. Anyone who forgot a knife, I have extras."

He glanced at Bree. She'd been quiet the whole way. Now wasn't the time to dig about Philip and why he was here. Bree hadn't looked surprised or too pleased. She'd once said that Philip had tried to talk Bree out of going to Seattle. Honestly, Darren couldn't blame him. Darren had wanted to do the same thing, but holding a person back never worked.

Stepping toward the rear of the van, he watched as Philip made a show of turning his Cadillac around before parking it a car length behind them, but faced the way they'd come in. He got out and then helped Joan. The guy leaned against the driver's side door when Bree went over there.

Darren could barely hear them, but he thought he heard Philip say something about relocating. To be near Bree. And Darren's gut twisted. He couldn't hear Bree's response or see her expression with her back to him, but those pretty shoulders of hers looked tense.

The urge to knock the arrogant smirk off that guy's face burned hot. Darren blew out his breath and opened the dual doors at the back of the van. He grabbed the box containing the red whistles and extra paring knives, then turned to the proper page in their wild edibles pamphlet and held it up. Instruction time.

"This is going to be pretty easy. Wild asparagus looks pretty much the same as domestic. There will be stalks growing along that fence line. There are pictures of what the mature ferns look like in your booklet, so you can look for them later in the year. To get new sprouts, the old stalks have to be cut down this time of year. I did this about a week ago. Anyone is welcome to come back in a few days and check for more. But do not cross the fence line, as that's private property. Please be considerate and make sure everyone has cut a few stalks before going back for more. I have another field prepped after this one."

Everyone scattered.

Philip walked toward him. The guy was dressed in khakis and a patterned button-down shirt. Not nearly as tall but slender, Philip approached with a slink to his step and held out a hand. "Joan tells me you're quite the outdoorsman."

Not a compliment. Darren shook the guy's soft hand anyway. "Yeah."

"Can you really eat this stuff?" Philip's lips curled into a half smile.

Bree had dated this pompous idiot? Darren caught her gaze.

She rolled her eyes as if he'd spoken the thought aloud. Then she turned to her mom. "Do you want me to pick for you?"

Joan limped forward, leaning on her cane. "No. I want to see what it looks like."

Darren could easily envision mother and daughter taking a tumble on the incline of the ditch and offered Joan his arm. "The next spot might be better for you since the ground is more level. We won't be here long."

"Oh." Joan hooked her elbow around his and waved off her daughter as they crossed the uneven dirt road. "You go ahead."

Bree hesitated a moment, watching Philip.

"I'll hang here and check my messages." Philip strolled back to his car and climbed in.

Darren watched Bree. She nearly slid down the ditch, intent on catching up with Stella. The two women spoke softly as they cut stalks side by side and moved on. He could only imagine what Stella said. She'd cast a couple of disgusted looks toward the blue coupe.

On the other side of the road, Joan let go of his arm. "Philip comes up every year, usually around the Fourth of July, with his folks. Our families have been friends for years. He's decided to move out west, too. I sure hope they get back together."

Not what Darren wanted to hear, but not surprising

that Joan would prefer the golden boy over him. Darren wouldn't ever be on Joan's list of eligible bachelors for her daughter. His salary, even with the field supervisor promotion to sergeant, wouldn't come close to what Philip pulled in.

"Does Bree want that?"

"They've broken up before, so we'll see. He's got a good future. Security and all."

"Right." What else could he say? Bree hadn't mentioned that they'd called it quits only to get back together. She hadn't been real talkative about this guy or the issues they'd had. But then he hadn't been a fountain of information about Raleigh either.

He stopped at the edge of the ditch with Bree's mom so they could watch everyone cutting spears of wild asparagus. He glanced at the Cadillac and Philip. Darren drove an old pick-up truck.

"Would you look at that?" Joan exclaimed. "That looks just like real asparagus."

"It is real, just not cultivated." His defenses rose.

Joan looked through him, catching the hidden meaning he hadn't meant to make. "You mean planted."

Darren glanced at Bree. She was cultivated, groomed for success and with her focus and talent, she'd succeed. He had no doubt about that. Whether fishing for smelt, cleaning them, scouring the woods for morels or playing her cello, Bree gave her all. But not her heart. She didn't want to make room in there for him. Was that because the golden boy still cornered the market there?

"I think that's it." Stella climbed up from the ditch, her little basket loaded with green spears and even some that trailed wispy branches.

"How's it look, Ed?" Darren had gotten used to checking with Ed before wrapping things up. The guy loved it.

"I think she's right. We got most all of it." Ed sheathed the machete knife.

Several of the other women were climbing up onto the road as well, comparing their finds. A few picked some spindly-looking daisies and pink clusters that grew along the road in clumps. Nothing on the protected list. Common wildflowers.

Bree came up last after holding on to everyone else's baskets. At the top, she stumbled. Her basket teetered and a few spears fell out.

Darren picked them up and offered them back.

"Thanks." Bree dragged her fingers across his palm, scooping up the stalks.

His gaze lingered on her apple-colored lips. He knew the softness there, the sweet taste. How long would it take to forget the feel of her kiss? The warmth of her embrace. "You're welcome."

She stared back, her golden eyes dark and stormy. Was she thinking the same thing?

"Ready to go?"

"Yes." Soft as a whisper, Bree walked past him and climbed into the passenger seat of the van.

She looked like a woman in turmoil, alright.

She wasn't the only one. He might have shown her what lay off the beaten path, but she'd walked right into his heart and made a mess there.

Chapter Twelve

The next field wasn't far away. Bree took in the beauty of a vast meadow dotted with daisies and Lake Michigan shining as a sparkling blue ribbon in the distance. She sighed. The view didn't matter, not when Philip's relocation announcement stole away her peace. What was he thinking, doing something like that?

She couldn't tell Philip where to live and work, but she could draw the line when it came to her. She'd let him edge his way back into her life before because they'd known each other a long time. Because their families were friends and wanted them together. But this time, they were through. She was done.

Bree glanced at her mother. With Darren's steadying hand, her mom sliced an asparagus spear and then plunked it in her basket. Bree should have been honest with her parents when it came to Philip, especially her mother.

"When do you leave?" Philip followed her.

She swallowed irritation and focused on the ground. "Soon."

"I can help you drive out and then fly back. Use it as an office space scouting trip."

"I'm good. I don't need your help." Bree cut a thick, short stalk of asparagus.

Philip stepped in front of her. "You can do your thing and I can expand my business. It'll be perfect."

Bree straightened to face him. "Breaking up wasn't only about the music residency."

His brown eyes narrowed. "Sure it was."

"I'm not interested in getting back together." She forced herself not to look away.

"Is this about him?" Philip gave a nod toward Darren.

"No." Bree was firm in her answer. It was none of Philip's business anyway. "This is about me and what I want for my future. We don't want the same things."

"Playing in that grungy coffee house wasn't safe—"

"Yes, it was. But it wasn't really the location, was it? You were—" Bree stopped.

He stepped closer. "Suppose you tell me what I was?"

He was a host of things she shouldn't put up with. He'd tried to dictate what she did or didn't do. She'd been perfectly safe in that coffee house, but Philip didn't like that she went somewhere he didn't want to go. Nor did he like the young composer she'd tried to help develop.

She shook her head. He'd never listened before. Why would he now? "I'm not going there. What matters is that I don't want you in my life."

There. She'd finally said it without flinching.

The steely look in Philip's eyes showed he struggled with hearing her, struggled to rein in his temper. One more reason she regretted a relationship with him. His fuse was much too short.

She made a move to step past him, but Philip blocked her path. Bree swallowed hard. "We're done."

"I don't think we are." His voice was softer than usual.

He sounded perfectly calm, almost as if he joked with her, but there was an edge she'd never heard before.

One look in his eyes and Bree shivered. She stepped back.

Philip laughed, spreading his arms wide in surrender. "You're so touchy."

Bree searched his face, but the odd fury was gone. She didn't wait for it to come back and slipped past him. Her fingers shook when she bent to cut the spear of asparagus she'd nearly stepped on. Settling the wild veggie in her basket, she moved closer to her mother.

"Here, you take these." She dumped her basket into her mother's. "I'll go get more."

"There's enough for dinner tonight. I invited Philip to stay with us." Her mom stepped forward to pick another green spear.

"Not a good idea, Mom."

"Why not?"

Bree briefly closed her eyes. They needed to have a talk, but not here. No way could she let Philip stay for dinner or anything else. She'd planned to leave early in the morning and didn't want Philip following her. Didn't want Philip staying behind when her father wasn't up north yet, either. "Trust me on this."

"It'll be fine." Her mother limped away to slice another spear. Her mom did pretty well with her cane. She'd be even stronger by next week's class.

"You okay?" Darren whispered.

Bree jumped. "Fine."

She watched Philip hold the basket for her mother while she bent and sliced the tender stalks of green. Bree needed to make him leave. She'd ride back to town with him. With her mom there, she'd spell it all out if she had to. Whatever it took.

"You sure?" Darren's voice sounded harsh. He looked like a bull ready to charge if she said the word.

The last thing Bree wanted was a scene. She laid her hand on his arm. "Please. It's fine."

But it wasn't. Bree had never felt this rattled before. Maybe she'd imagined that dark look in Philip's eyes. But what if she hadn't?

Something didn't feel right. Darren wasn't sure if it was his jealousy kicking in or if Philip might be a wolf in sheep's clothing. Very expensive clothing. He'd be all over the guy if needed, but Bree had said she was fine. Philip stayed near Joan, away from Bree.

"Aren't you going to do something about that?" Stella poked him with her elbow.

"About what?" Darren sliced an asparagus stalk.

"Philip," Stella whispered through her teeth. "He's moving out there."

Darren couldn't keep a guy from relocating. "I heard."

Stella stared him down.

"What?"

"You're better for Bree."

"Thanks for your vote, but that's up to her, now, isn't it?"

Stella poked him again. "So? Go out there and see her."

"Seattle's not exactly across the pond."

Stella shook her head. "Youth is wasted on the young."

"What's that supposed to mean, anyway?"

"It means you're seeing only obstacles and not possibilities. Don't lose her to distance, Darren. She cares for you."

"Hmm." There was no right reply to such a comment.

He knew that Bree didn't want to care. She didn't want a relationship between them to get in the way of her plans. If she got back with Philip because he was willing to move near her, there wasn't much he could do about it. He wasn't getting into that position again. Losing out to golden boy success.

There wasn't much he could do to gain Joan's approval, either. Not when the woman wanted Bree and Philip back together. A family's opinion carried a lot of weight when it came to relationships. Mothers knew if a guy wasn't good enough for their daughters. Unless that mother didn't really know her own daughter.

He turned to Stella. "How well do you know this guy?"

Stella shrugged. "Well enough to know that I don't like him. Bree broke up with him once before but took him back."

"What happened?"

Stella shrugged. "I'm not sure. She never talked much about it."

He should stop digging and talk to Bree. Relationships were an odd place of discovery. Sometimes it took a while to realize why things didn't work. He checked his watch. Their class time was spent. "Okay, everyone, let's load up."

"'Bout time. My bag is near bursting." Ed made his usual grumbles. His plastic grocery bag was indeed packed full. Ed's thinning dark hair had been blown out of place by the wind, and holding that long field knife made him look like an old pirate. All Ed was missing was the black patch over one eye.

Darren laughed.

"What's so funny?" Ed didn't look amused.

"That's some knife." Darren slapped Ed on the back.

"My daughter gave it to me for Christmas." The old man sheathed it with a scowl.

"Good gift." He nodded and counted heads as they loaded into the van. Six, seven, eight, nine—Bree made ten, but she hesitated before climbing in.

"Joan's riding back with me in case I get turned around." Philip thumbed toward his Cadillac. He'd already started the slick coupe, no doubt to kick in the air conditioning.

"Hang on and I'll go with you." Bree handed Darren her basket. It overflowed with green spears and leggy stalks. "Can you take this for me? I'll see you back at the community room."

"No problem." He took the small basket, covered her hands and searched her face. "Everything okay?"

She wouldn't meet his eyes but gave his hand a quick squeeze. "See you in a few."

He watched her dart toward Philip's coupe.

Philip held the driver's seat forward for her to climb into the back while Joan tried opening the passenger door without success.

"It's locked." Joan tried it again. "Philip?"

"I'll get it in a minute." Philip's smooth voice sounded more like a shrill growl.

He'd only met the guy today, but that voice didn't sound right. Philip sounded nervous.

The hairs on his arms itched with a tingling sensation Darren knew all too well. He set Bree's basket down and walked toward the idling car. He was used to acting on hunches, but his mind raced for an excuse to get the women back in the van.

Before Darren took more than five steps, Philip had slipped behind the wheel and driven off without Joan.

Fast.

Dust kicked up from behind the car, which tore down the road, its back end fishtailing on the packed dirt.

"Philip!" Joan nearly fell as she quickly backed up.

Darren steadied her shoulders. "Get to the van."

She coughed but didn't move. "Why—"

"Now, Joan." Darren's instincts took over. He could

barely make out the license plate through the cloud of dust, but managed to memorize some of it and quickly jotted it down.

Joan stood gaping after the speeding car. "Why would he do that?"

Darren called Bree's cell and got voice mail. "Call me."

Something was definitely wrong. He wrapped his arm around Joan's shoulders and quickly led her back to the van. "What's Philip's last name?"

"Ah…let me think." She shook her head as if trying to clear it before climbing in. "I've known them for years, why can't I think… Johnson!" Joan's face paled. "Do you think he *took* her?"

"Maybe." Seemed pretty obvious after the way he'd left Joan. The woman could have been hurt.

Joan gasped, and her shoulders quivered with a sob ready to roll out. She looked like she was about to crumple into a heap but blathered on. "It's my fault for letting him come up. I thought if Bree saw him again, they could work things out."

He touched her arm. "Hang with me, Joan, okay? We'll figure this out." He sounded more confident than he felt. His instincts screamed that Philip had kidnapped Bree. His hand tightened around his cell. If he was wrong—

Deep down, he knew he wasn't.

Philip Johnson. Could the name be more common? Searching for such a common name to match what little he had of a plate number would be slow. He quickly texted Bree and waited a couple of seconds. Nothing. Not even a smiley face or question marks.

Nothing.

Darren's blood ran cold.

Stella popped down from inside the van and helped Joan into the passenger seat. "Buckle up, now. That's it."

He gave her a grateful nod with his phone to his ear.

"Let's go after him, Darren." Stella stood with hands on hips.

As if he could. He had no idea what direction Philip had gone. He'd waste time driving aimlessly and couldn't do that with a van full of civilians. If Philip had truly taken Bree against her will—and that fact hadn't firmly been established yet—Darren needed to tread with care. Philip struck him as the kind of guy who'd sue at the drop of a hat. He'd been awfully jumpy right before taking off. Was that when he planned this...

"What are we waiting for?"

"Yeah, let's go." Echoes of agreement came from the rest of them. Ed had even pulled out that knife.

"Put that thing away before someone gets hurt," Stella yelled as she climbed back into the van.

An argument ensued, and Darren raised his hand to quiet them as he made another phone call. "Stan? It's Darren. A situation might be developing, and I need to trade vehicles. Meet me in front of the Bayside General Store. I'm less than ten minutes away. Good."

Darren climbed behind the wheel and started the engine. "Buckle up and hang on. This is going to be a rough ride."

"Let's go get Bree," Connie called out.

More bluster from his elderly avengers.

In other circumstances, he might have laughed. Ideally, when this was over, he could have a good laugh with Bree. His gut twisted. He didn't have a good feeling about this, though, and his hunches were usually right.

Turning the van around on the narrow dirt road, Darren glanced at Bree's mom. She gripped her cane tight. So tight, her fingers looked white. "It's going to be okay."

Joan's eyes were wet, but she'd calmed down. Her face remained pale. "He won't hurt her. He's crazy about her."

Or plain crazy.

The occupants in the van quieted as reality hit. Bree was in danger. How serious the danger was yet to be determined. As he tore down the dirt road with the windows open, dust sifted in and choked off conversation.

He glanced at his phone lying in the console next to him. *Come on, Bree. Give me something here. Are you okay?*

A few minutes later, Darren's phone buzzed to life with a text, and his heart stopped when he read it.

M ID V Rd. HEL

He grabbed his phone and called for backup. "Looking for a newish bright blue Cadillac coupe registered to a Philip Johnson last on Middle Village Road. Looks like an abduction."

He heard the sharp intake of Joan's breath.

That sound tore through him as he pulled into the parking lot of a little old general store in the middle of nowhere.

Darren was out of the van and heading for his fellow CO's truck in seconds. "Take these people back to Bay Willows. I'm going after Johnson."

Stan nodded and tossed him the keys.

Darren caught them and turned back to Joan. She looked so small and sick with worry in the passenger seat. "I'll find her. I'll bring Bree back."

Joan nodded, trying to be brave. It was then that he saw the resemblance Bree had to her mom. That willingness to stretch and conquer fear.

Fear for Bree's safety cut through him. He prayed that he'd find her quickly. And he prayed he'd find her safe.

"Philip! Slow down." Bree tried to climb into the front seat, but Philip pushed her back. She slammed hard against the leather seat. "What's wrong with you? Stop this car right now!"

He didn't say a word.

She looked out the back window. Already they were far away, speeding down the road. Through the cloud of dust, she spotted Darren with her mother leaning against him. She could have been hurt by Philip tearing away like he had. Tears stung the corners of her eyes.

Mom.

She heard her cell phone's muffled ringtone. It had to be Darren. She reached for her phone but came up empty. She searched the floor, the seat. Nothing. It must have fallen out of her pocket.

"Don't answer that," Philip growled.

Her phone kept ringing, making her frantic. "I can't even find it. Will you please stop the car?"

"Shut up!" His shrill voice slapped her ears.

She looked at his reflection in the rearview mirror. Philip had a wild look in his eyes that she didn't like. Didn't trust, either. She quickly scanned the floor, felt under the front seats. Nothing. "Where are we going?"

"Someplace to talk."

"There's nothing more to say—" Her phone buzzed with an incoming text. Where was it?

"You wouldn't return my calls or my texts. I had to come up here so you'd see."

"See what?" Bree felt along the crease in the back-seat. Her fingers connected with the plastic rhinestone-encrusted case. Slowly she pulled it out, keeping it low so Philip wouldn't see.

Darren had texted her.

"That we belong together. We always have."

No, they didn't. Bree knew the moment he'd freaked over her application to the music residency that she needed to get out of their relationship once and for all. Philip had gone on a rant, saying he wouldn't allow it.

At the time, she'd nearly laughed because he'd acted like her nephew during one of his temper tantrums. She'd thought Philip couldn't have been serious. Like an idiot, Bree had believed his excuse of stress for the bizarre behavior. Right now he was acting the same way. Oh, why hadn't she told her parents then?

Quieting her voice, she tried again. "Stop the car, let me get in the front seat and then we can talk."

"No."

Bree searched the vast fields and wooded hills beyond. Where were they? They'd driven onto pavement, and Philip floored it. There were no street signs that she could see. She hit Reply, focusing on where they might be so she could tell Darren as soon as she knew something. Anything.

"I'll do the thinking for both us. You just stay quiet back there," Philip barked.

Bree racked her brain. Glancing around the car's interior, she knew she had to find a way to escape and fast. They came to an intersection, and Bree peered out the side window. She spotted a green road sign. Elated, she typed the street name into her phone while keeping it low, out of Philip's sight. She hit Send, hoping it made sense.

"Give me that." Philip reached for her phone.

She wrestled away from him. "Stop it."

The car jerked sideways, nearly going off the road as Philip grabbed her hair and pulled hard.

"Ow!" She dropped her phone to grab his hand.

He pushed her back again. Harder this time. "Don't make me hurt you."

The tone of his voice stopped her cold. Would he really

hurt her? Up until this point, she hadn't thought him capable. She'd known him for years. Surely he wouldn't…

She glanced at him again in the rearview mirror.

Philip stared back. He didn't look right. "Don't think I won't."

"Why?" It came out a raw whisper. "Why are you doing this?"

His feverish gaze shifted to the road ahead of them. "I saw how that guy looked at you."

Darren.

"We're friends, Philip. That's all." Bree appealed to his common sense, but this wasn't a jealous fit. Philip had been jealous of the young composer. Philip had been many things, but never crazy.

This was crazy.

Bree closed her eyes and prayed. *Dear Lord, please get me out of this. Please help Darren find me.*

Philip took a turn. According to the dashboard, they headed north. "I won't let him have you."

"Where are we going?" she croaked.

"You'll see."

She searched the floor for her phone. It lay under the passenger seat. Reaching for it, she dialed 911.

Philip's hand swooped down and grabbed it. She pulled at his arm, but he jerked away, pressed the button to open his window and threw it out.

"No!" Bree turned and watched it bounce once, twice, three times before it lay along the narrow, sandy shoulder of the road. Her only connection to Darren now gone.

Her stomach twisted. She mopped the sweat that beaded along her hairline with shaky fingers.

Find me, Darren. Please find me.

The window remained open and the warm air whipped

in, beating up her now throbbing head and tossing her hair in all directions. She had to think.

Think!

They were miles from town but no longer in the desolate area they'd come from. Though sparse, there were houses on this road. Even a couple of farms. The surroundings looked familiar, too. She'd been on this road before. Last week on the way to the Zelinsky home, she'd followed the van.

Her pulse picked up speed.

She had to do something fast before Philip pulled off somewhere. Before he made good on his threat to hurt her. Somehow she had to get out of this car.

Bree stared at the road ahead. There was a sharp turn somewhere on this road that Darren had warned her about. She remembered slowing down… Had they already passed it? No. She spotted a big old farmhouse up ahead, and her memory sharpened into focused clarity. That curve was coming up soon.

She buckled into the backseat belt and loosened it. She'd need some give in order to make this work. Biting her lip till it bled, she leaned forward enough to see how fast Philip drove. She couldn't see over his shoulder, but she could reach down to the button that controlled the position of his seat.

"You have to slow down," she yelled.

"Not till we're there."

"But there's a curve up ahead, and you won't make it if you keep driving this fast."

He let up a little, but not much, and slightly turned his head. "Don't mess with me."

"I'm not." She clicked the lever to move the seat forward.

Philip swore and slammed on the brakes. "What are you doing?"

She kept pushing that seat forward even as Philip tried to bat her hand away. The car swerved and he overcompensated, sending the car out of control.

They flew off the road, and it felt like they went airborne, floating for a second or two. But it was enough time to let go.

Bree grasped her knees, tucking herself into an airline crash position she'd seen in movies.

They hit hard. Her head slammed into the back of Philip's seat before she was thrown hard against her own.

Through the haze of Philip's curses, she heard grass and clumps of dirt whipping against the bottom of the car as they continued too fast through the field. The deafening sound made her head spin.

Then they stopped with a jarring crunch of metal, a shuddering thud that made her teeth chatter as she flew forward once again. The seat belt bit into her belly, making her heave. Her forehead hit the corner of the driver's seat and she saw stars.

In that flash of sparkling darkness, the last thing Bree heard was the poof of a deployed airbag and Philip's pained groan.

Chapter Thirteen

Darren drove east on Middle Village Road. No sign of Philip's Cadillac. Not that he expected to see it. Darren was a good fifteen minutes behind them. Too much could happen in fifteen minutes.

What if he hurts her?

Darren pulled over. Scanning the open fields and tree line beyond, he pushed those what-ifs out of his head before he lost it. He focused on entering Bree's cell phone number into the laptop and waited for the tracking program to locate it. He'd find them. No matter what, he'd find them.

State Road. He called in that they'd headed north and he was in pursuit.

He prayed again for Bree's safety.

As for Philip's...he wanted to rip that guy apart.

Taking off fast, Darren heard his tires squeal on pavement. He glanced at the screen, but Bree's cell still showed the same location. He made the turn onto State and drove a mile or so, but no vehicles were in sight. He caught a flash of something shiny on the side of the road and pulled over once again.

It was Bree's phone on the ground. He picked up the sparkly case and bounced it against the palm of his hand.

He had nothing to go on now. He kicked the truck's tire before climbing back in.

Chatter over the wire confirmed two units were heading north as well. The state police and the county sheriff's department were involved. His gut clenched when he heard the announcement that Philip's Cadillac had been reported in a crash with airbags deployed by the vehicle's security system.

Cold fear clamped down hard as he heard the location. He knew exactly where they'd gone off the road. He got on the wire and announced he was only minutes south and on his way.

His hands gripped the steering wheel until they hurt. He knew the sharp curve on that road. His thoughts raced faster than his driving. What would he find?

God, please keep her safe.

When he finally pulled off the road before that deadly curve, what he saw made him believe God had answered his prayer. The Cadillac was upright and slammed head-on into a small tree. The front end was crumpled in, but the windshield remained intact. It was amazing that the coupe hadn't flipped and rolled.

He heard sirens in the distance as he ran toward the vehicle, still idling with a chug, chug and clanging sound. Steam poured out from under the hood. He reached into the open driver's side window and pushed Philip back against the seat. He looked dazed, mumbling.

"Where is she?" Darren scanned the interior of the coupe. No Bree.

"Can't have her." Philip's nose was swollen and red. Darren hoped it was broken.

He grabbed the guy's shirt collar. "Where's Bree?"

"I don't know."

Darren let go and Philip slumped over. He turned off the

engine and reached for the trunk release. Hearing it pop, he went behind the car and searched. The only thing in there was a fancy duffel bag. Darren didn't bother opening it.

Slamming the trunk, he turned around and scanned the horizon, finally spotting her in a field.

Bree ran, tripped and fell. She got up again and ran some more toward a house set way back from the road. Smart girl. She was going for help. And too far away to hear him if he yelled.

Darren ran back to his truck, jumped in and drove off the road into the field with teeth-rattling speed, beeping the horn as he went. The truck bounced over ruts, but he didn't let up on the gas.

Bree stopped running. She looked straight at him and crumpled to the ground.

Darren slammed the truck into Park and got out at a run. His throat closed up tight, making it difficult to speak. He knelt down and gathered Bree into his arms, whispering, "It's over."

Bree hung on tight, sobbing.

He stroked her hair, pulling out bits of dried grass, and kissed her forehead. A lump had formed there. She needed medical attention; they were no doubt on the way, signaled by the deployed airbags. He cradled her close, breathing in her scent. She smelled like the outdoors, like spring air and sunshine. His Bree. "I've got you. I've got you…"

"I knew you'd find me," she choked out. "I prayed that you would."

He held her tighter, trying to ease the trembling that wracked her delicate frame. Hoping to cease his own shaking. He'd never felt so helpless before. He could have lost her. She could have been killed if that car—

Darren refused to think about that now. He pulled back and searched her face and body. Other than the goose-egg on her forehead, scratches on her arms and legs and a puffy dark mark on her shin that had the makings of an ugly bruise, she looked whole.

He brushed hair away from her lips. "Where else are you hurt?"

She shook her head. "Just sore, nothing serious."

"What happened?"

"I couldn't talk sense into Philip. He was crazy and wouldn't stop the car. I remembered this road from when we went to your parents' house, so I waited for the curve. Then I messed with his seat trying to distract him enough to slow down, get him to stop—" Her bottom lip trembled.

He brushed his lips over hers, featherlight in case even that hurt. Kissing her was killing him right along with thoughts of how badly that crash could have ended.

When she deepened the kiss with the same desperation, he pulled her even closer. Grateful for this brave girl, his heart broke with every breath and every murmur.

The sirens sounded closer. He opened his eyes and spotted the flashing lights from the police and emergency responders drawing near, pulling off the road.

He cupped her face. "We've got to go."

"No." Bree didn't move. Her brow furrowed and she gripped his forearms.

He gently pulled her up with him. "I'm right here. I won't leave you."

She clung to his hand until she climbed into the truck.

He offered her phone. "The police will want to see this, but you should call your mom. Let her know you're okay."

She nodded. Her face streaked with dried tears, she hit a couple of buttons and connected. "Mom?" Her voice wavered. "No. I'm okay. Darren found me. I'm with him now. The police are here, too."

He reached for her hand and felt her tremble again.

Her eyes filled with new tears that ran down her cheeks. "No. No. Philip didn't hurt me."

He could have.

Darren felt sick with relief. This could have been worse. Much worse. The urge to rip that guy apart washed over him anew. He grasped the steering wheel with both hands, squeezing tight. Would Bree press charges? Maybe she wouldn't have to.

He could arrest the guy, but knew he shouldn't. He couldn't be objective and didn't want his feelings for Bree to come back and bite him. He'd give the police a statement and let them handle it. They'd have enough to haul Philip to jail.

Bree sat on a gurney in the back of the ambulance while a paramedic examined her. Through the open doors, she watched as Philip was questioned by police and then taken into custody. She clutched the edge of that gurney hard, fighting wooziness.

She'd gotten him arrested.

Bree blew out her breath. No, that wasn't right. Philip had made his own choices by coming here. He'd taken hers away by not letting her go. Her heart pounded hard, like when she woke from a bad dream. Her head hurt and her muscles were sore. She wanted to go, get away from all of this. Now.

Darren spoke with another state trooper and gave her a hint of a smile. The same smile he'd given her when they'd eaten s'mores in front of a crackling fire in his home. The image beckoned her to return there, safe and sound. But that wasn't home. It couldn't be.

The paramedics quit prodding and poking, satisfied that she had nothing worse than a mild concussion. Nothing a good amount of rest wouldn't cure. They'd nixed her idea of leaving for Seattle in the morning, stating she was in no condition to drive cross-country.

"Can I please go now?"

"In a minute." The state trooper who'd been talking to Darren stood before her. "I need to ask you a few questions."

Her gaze flew to Darren's.

He slipped next to her, grabbed her hand and squeezed. "Just tell him what happened."

Bree swallowed hard against nausea and retold the story.

The whole time, she thought about Philip's parents and how they'd react when they heard the news that their son had been arrested. Because of her. Would their business suffer? Would anyone back home find out? Would they care?

Would their parents remain friends? Doubtful. Her stomach pitched. It'd be easier on everyone if she let this incident go, but she'd let too much go unnoticed for too long.

"He didn't hurt me." The memory of Philip pulling her hair flashed through her mind. If they hadn't crashed, would he have really hurt her?

She closed her eyes, searching for direction. What was the right thing to do here?

"You gave your consent to go with him. Is that right?" the trooper clarified.

She opened her eyes. "Yes. I didn't want my mother to ride alone with him."

"And why was that?" He jotted down notes.

Bree looked at Darren.

He gave her an encouraging nod, but his expression was closed. He was leaving it up to her how much to tell or not tell. He gave her the power instead of taking over and talking for her.

Time to be heard. She took a deep breath. "He's been harassing me ever since we broke up with constant texts and calls…"

Bree explained everything she knew. Philip showing up to tell her about his plans to relocate, the creepy feeling she got when he wouldn't let her pass by him earlier and even how Philip had been jealous of Darren. She also gave permission to check her cell phone records.

The state trooper didn't look a bit shocked.

It all felt foreign to Bree as she explained how Philip had tried to mold her into what *he* wanted while they'd dated. Subtly at first, until he wouldn't let her be who she was. He fought against her dreams and ambitions, but he'd never been crazy like this.

She'd tried breaking things off with him once before, but his pleas to get back together had been persuasive. Their families had been, too. Feeling trapped, the music residency had come at a perfect time, when she'd needed a clean break with distance.

"Anything else you can add?"

Bree gripped Darren's hand tighter. "That's pretty much everything."

The trooper snapped shut his notebook. "We'll contact you if we need anything else."

"I'm still leaving for Seattle in a couple of days." Bree could hardly wait to get away and put this far behind her.

"Noted. We have your number."

"Thank you." Bree followed Darren to the big black DNR truck.

He held the door open for her. "Isn't that a little early to leave?"

She climbed into the passenger seat. "Nope. I want out of here."

The ride back to Maple Springs was a quiet one. She glanced at Darren and the hard set of his jaw and wanted to cry. The truck's console equipped with a laptop and radio stood between them, but soon they'd have half a country separating them. She'd miss him. Surely, he'd miss her too. Wouldn't he?

Almost to Maple Springs, Darren pulled off into an elementary school parking lot on the edge of town, cut the engine and turned in his seat.

Her stomach dipped and rolled.

He searched her face. "Thank you for helping out with the wild edibles class."

Bree's eyes burned. "You're welcome."

He looped her hair behind her ear. "I mean it, Bree. You've helped me face a few things about myself. The way I view people. The way I view you."

She swallowed hard as tears ran down her cheeks. This sounded a lot like a goodbye speech.

"You'll be surrounded by your family, and that's good. You need them now. Give yourself some time to get through this before leaving. You did the right thing today by telling the police what's been going on. You're a brave woman, Bree."

"It didn't feel right or good," she whispered. It was all she could manage around the tightness of her throat.

"I know. I'm proud of how you handled yourself. Using your head may have saved your life."

Her chin shook and then her shoulders.

"Aww, Bree, please don't cry."

She covered her face with her hands. "I'm sorry."

Darren got out of the truck, walked around and opened her door. "Come on, sweet. Don't do this."

She sobbed harder when he lifted her into his arms and shifted into the passenger seat. He settled her onto his lap, cradling her close. "It's going to be okay."

It didn't feel okay.

What if she had to testify? Philip would make bail, and

then what if he came after her again? She leaned into Darren's broad chest, spent. "I want to go."

Darren kissed her temple. "I don't want you to. Stay here. Stay with me."

Her heart pinched with temptation to accept. He was safe and strong. But she couldn't spend every day glued to his side. She pulled back and searched his face. "I can't."

"Yes, you can."

She closed her eyes. "Please don't."

"We have something here. Why let that go?"

Kate had said that if their feelings were real, they'd keep. But could they really keep for two years? Everything had an expiration date if left unattended for too long. Visiting only a couple of times in between might spoil an otherwise decent friendship. Unless…

Bree threw down the gauntlet. "Come with me. They must have conservation officers out there, too."

Darren's face fell.

In that one look, Bree knew he wouldn't. He couldn't. Neither of them wanted to risk their dreams on an untried relationship. Darren loved this area too much to leave it. He wanted the supervisor position that would only entrench him further in this county. His home. She'd known that from the start. She didn't blame him. In fact, she understood. Perfectly.

"Now you know how I feel," she whispered.

He nodded, looking exhausted. "Yeah. I do, and I'm sorry."

"Me, too."

The thing about vacations was knowing when they were over.

Darren pulled into the drive in front of the Anderson cottage. He wouldn't linger. Bree needed to be with her family right now. With Joan. A place he didn't belong.

Bree opened the door but didn't get out. "Come in with me?"

"I'd better not."

"Please."

She'd been through a lot today, and yet he'd pressed her to stay in Michigan. As much as it hurt to hear her refuse him, he was proud of her resolve. Proud of her commitment. It was something he understood.

He spotted Joan standing under the porch light with her cane in hand. "But your mom—"

"Will want to thank you. I'm not getting out until you do." Bree lifted her chin.

He blew out his breath and rubbed the back of his neck before climbing out of the truck. He met Bree on the sidewalk. "Only for a minute."

She grabbed his hand.

He threaded his fingers through hers and squeezed. When they stepped up on the porch, he could tell that Joan had been crying. Her eyes looked puffy and her face was red. Despite her uppity ways, she didn't deserve the frantic worry she'd been put through. He couldn't imagine the guilt she must feel knowing she'd been so wrong about the golden boy.

Bree ran into her mother's arms.

"Your father's on his way." Mother clung to daughter. "Your sister, too. She wants to drive with you to Seattle, and I won't let you refuse."

Bree nodded.

Darren shifted his stance. He was glad Bree wouldn't be alone on that long trek. Very glad. But it was time to go. Time to let her go, too. He stepped back.

Joan glanced at him as if she'd forgotten he was there. She extended her hand. "Thank you, Darren. Thank you for bringing her home safe and sound."

Darren cleared his throat as he gripped her hand, shocked when she pulled him toward their embrace. He gave both women a brief hug. "Your daughter never lost her cool, and that made a huge difference."

"I knew you'd find me," Bree added.

"Darren, please come in." Joan kept her arm around Bree's shoulders.

"I've got to go. This truck belongs to another CO." He didn't belong here. He couldn't rehash this afternoon with two women in tears. Besides, he and Bree had said everything that needed saying. The longer he hung around, the harder it would be not to beg. He wanted Bree to stay but understood why she couldn't.

Joan nodded. "Come this weekend, then. The whole family will be here to give Bree a proper send-off."

Bree looked at him but didn't press.

"I'll think about it." Darren's skin itched thinking about it. This was Bree's world, not his.

"We'd be honored." Joan gave him an encouraging smile that softened her face, erasing the pinched look he'd often seen before. That disapproving look was gone, too.

"Mom, go on inside. I'll be there in a minute." Bree practically pushed her mother into the house before turning back to him.

He backed up, taking a step down off the porch. It brought him eye to eye with Bree. He wanted to touch her but kept his hands at his sides.

"Thank you," Bree whispered. Her pretty eyes were puffy and red-rimmed. "For everything."

His throat felt tight. "You're welcome."

She cupped his face and kissed him hard.

He kissed her back, clenching his hands into fists to keep from drawing her too close. Too close to ever let go. Darren had to let her go. This was goodbye.

Bree pulled back and rested her hands on his shoulders. "Text me? I want to know how you do with that promotion."

"Okay, sure." He backed down another step.

Bree gave him a watery smile and then went inside.

Through the windows, he saw Joan wrap her into another hug. Darren walked away with a heavy heart.

Two years was a long time. Too long.

Memorial Day, Darren found himself paired with his father in a game of horseshoes. A family tradition, but Darren's head wasn't in the game. Neither was his heart. He'd received a text from Bree that morning. She and her sister had made it to Seattle. She was settling into the dorm-like studio apartment that came with her residency and already loved the area.

She might as well have tied him to a block of cement and thrown him overboard. The tone of that text made it pretty clear that Bree wasn't coming back. He'd known from the start that she'd leave. So why'd he allow his feelings to grow into something that felt a lot like love? It sure stung like love.

Love beareth all things, believeth all things, hopeth all things, endureth all things.

He'd heard that as part of the message the previous morning. He'd attended the church where his brothers Zach and Matthew went. A community church with little of the traditional pomp he was used to. He'd listened, though. Listened hard.

God, what are You trying to tell me?

His father slapped him on the back. "Your turn."

"Huh? Oh. Yeah." Darren took the shoe and threw. It clanged against the cast-iron pin and then took a roll off to the side, landing in deep grass outside the lane of play.

"That's a horrible throw," Monica jeered.

Darren shrugged.

"Okay, who died?" Monica asked.

Cam pushed at her shoulder. "Give it a rest."

Monica pushed him back. "Give what a rest? I'm just asking."

Darren held the other shoe. "You two done?"

"If you don't land a ringer, you and Dad lose," Monica said. "And that'll make me and Erin the winners."

"Under duress. Darren's not in usual form," Cam said.

Monica grinned. "Still counts."

"Yeah, still counts." Erin looked at him with concern in her eyes. Big brown puppy eyes, he used to tease her. "You okay?"

Darren paused from throwing. "I'll live."

Erin shrugged. "I don't know. You seem really sad."

He chuckled. "I'll get over it."

"But will you get over her?" Cam asked.

That was the question. One he'd asked himself about a hundred times since dropping Bree off at her parents' cottage less than a week ago. His whole family knew Bree had left. They knew about her scare with Philip, too. The abduction had hit the local news. It was no wonder Bree had skipped out early, missing her family picnic.

Maybe they hadn't had one. He'd talked to Stella, and she hadn't said anything about the Andersons having a get-together. Maybe he'd swing by and check on her later in the week. Darren prepared to throw but his sister's voice intruded, knocking off his concentration once again.

"How's that poem go?" Erin mumbled a few lines. "Wait, I got it. If you love something, let it go. If it comes back to you, it's yours forever. If it doesn't, then it was never meant to be."

Cam groaned.

Darren did, too. "That's corny."

Erin smiled. "Don't you think she'll come back, even for a visit?"

Bree's family summered here. That didn't mean she'd want to come back for him. She'd texted him, though, and he hadn't yet replied.

"Your turn, son," his father reminded him.

Darren stalled as that simple command echoed through his soul. Maybe it was his turn to prove he was worthy to be loved. He needed to let go of past hurts and failures and be the man he needed to be. Supporting Bree, instead of trying to change her mind. Her dreams. He needed to text her back. Go visit her, even.

Their father shook his head. "Will you throw that shoe so we can go eat?"

Darren launched the cast-iron horseshoe. It arced high and landed with a metal-whirling-around-metal sound. Everyone hooted and hollered, but not Monica or Erin. They both groaned when he scored the win with a ringer.

Darren turned to his baby sister. "Looks like the win was never yours to keep."

"Ha, ha." Erin rolled her eyes.

As they made their way to the house, Darren turned that hokey little poem over in his head. He'd let Bree go, alright. But then, she needed to fly on her own before she'd ever be happy being his.

His grandmother had called dating "courtship." He'd had only a temporary courtship with Bree. Neither were ready for anything permanent. At least not yet. Both of them had work to do.

The scripture he'd heard rolled through his thoughts once again. Maybe it was time to trust that God would bring them together when the timing was right.

Chapter Fourteen

A month later

Darren entered the courtroom for Philip's preliminary examination. The idiot had stuck with his not guilty plea, so here they were, wasting time figuring out if this would go to trial. Darren hoped to spare Bree and her mom from that. He was an eyewitness for the prosecution. Surely his testimony would be enough for probable cause and seal the false imprisonment charges. If the defense was smart, they'd settle for a plea bargain.

Stepping toward the front, Darren spotted long mink-colored hair and froze. Bree was here. He hadn't expected to see her at this stage of the game. She hadn't said anything about it, but then they hadn't spoken or even texted in the last couple of weeks. Finally losing touch after only a month apart.

Darren had been promoted into the supervisor position he'd applied for. His boss had said that he'd received several recommendations from folks in Bay Willows. Darren finally had everything he'd wanted, but one thing remained out of touch. Across country.

He slipped quietly into the bench seat behind her and

her family. The wood creaked when he sat down, announcing his presence.

Joan turned and gave him a warm smile.

He nodded.

His cell phone vibrated with an incoming text. It came from Bree.

Talk later?

His heart lodged somewhere in his throat. He texted back.

Sure.

The hearing started, and sure enough, Bree was called to testify right after the arresting officer. Taking the stand, she didn't look at him. Darren wished that she would, for moral support at the very least, but not once did her gaze connect with his.

He couldn't look away. She seemed more confident than he remembered. She answered the questions with poise but not indifference. Recalling the events affected her, but she didn't cry. She didn't waver, either, staring Philip down until he looked away. That sent a message of its own. One Darren hoped hadn't escaped the eyes of the judge.

When the defense attorney cross-examined Bree, Darren gripped the edge of his seat until he thought his fingers might break. The urge to rip Philip and his fancy attorney apart surged hot through his veins, but Darren stayed quiet.

When Bree finally stepped down, she held her head high but still didn't look his way. Incredible since he sat right behind her. She avoided him but wanted to talk later. What did that mean?

His gut clenched. Had she found someone else?

He ran a hand through his hair. Feeling fidgety, Darren wiped his palms against his thighs, waiting for Philip to take the stand, but both attorneys approached the judge instead.

The three spoke too softly to hear, but Darren knew Philip was doomed. That guy couldn't defend himself, not against what Bree had told the court. The golden boy was guilty and rightfully tarnished.

Silence settled over the too warm courtroom, and Darren shifted. His empty gun holster tapped against the back of the bench with a resounding thwack that seemed to echo through the chamber.

Philip turned and glared at him.

Darren stared back.

The guy didn't look sorry. If anything, Philip seemed even more arrogant, finally looking away when his attorney returned to his side.

And then it was over. The defense accepted a misdemeanor plea. The judge sentenced Philip to twelve months of probation, anger management classes, a fine and orders to stay away from Bree. No contact whatsoever. No jail time, either, but considering this was Philip's first offense, Darren hadn't expected more.

While Bree and her family shook the prosecutor's hand, Darren made for the doors. He'd wait for them in the hallway.

He didn't have to wait long.

"Darren, how are you?" Bree's mom was the first to greet him with a warm hug. "This is my husband, Ron. Bree's father."

"I'm fine, Mrs. Anderson. Mr. Anderson." Darren offered his hand to Bree's father. "And how are you both?"

"Glad this is over. Why don't you come by the cottage later for dinner?"

Darren glanced at Bree.

"Please say you'll come?" Her smile flashed those dimples he'd missed.

He missed her, and without even thinking, he agreed. "Okay, sure."

"We'll see you at home," Joan said with a wave.

Bree's parents left, and she looked a little nervous. "There goes my ride."

Darren chuckled. They were the next town over. A little far for Bree to walk home. "Seriously?"

"Yes, seriously." Her dimples flashed deeper as she took in his sergeant badge. "How's your new job?"

"Good. I got several recommendations after that day. One from your mom. Did you know that?"

"Yes. She thinks you're very sharp." She looked up into his eyes. "Can we walk?"

Darren hesitated. Would this be good or bad?

Bree looked worried. "I mean, if you have time. You're on duty."

"I have time." He'd make time. All the time he could with her.

He held open the door for her, and they walked outside into the warm sunshine of late June. The sidewalks swarmed with tourists. With the Fourth of July falling on the upcoming weekend, this week and next would be the busiest of the season with the arrival of so many vacationers. He'd already had an active few days working with his COs on the bay, making sure boaters stayed sober and safe.

"You look impressive in that tie, by the way. Do you have to wear one now?"

"No. It's my dress uniform. I'm supposed to wear it every time I go to court. I'm surprised I wasn't asked to testify."

Bree glanced at him, and her golden eyes reflected the

sun. "I didn't want you to. Not if it wasn't needed. That's why I'm here instead of a written statement. I didn't want this to go to trial."

He stopped walking and faced her. "Why didn't you call me?"

Bree groaned. "I wanted to. But I was asked not to talk about the case. I knew if I called—texted, even—you might call back, and then I'd tell you everything. I was so scared that our relationship might get dragged into all this and hurt your new position. I didn't want your reputation questioned because you got involved with me while on duty."

He looped the ends of her hair around his fingers. "You didn't have to protect me. We've got nothing to hide or be sorry for. As my grandmother used to say, we were only courting."

"Is that so?" Bree laughed and ran her finger down the length of his tie. "And now what are we doing?"

He stilled her hand by covering it with his own. "That's up to you."

She looked up. "I miss you."

"I miss you, more than I thought possible." He pulled her to him.

"Oh, Darren, what are we going to do?"

Holding her close, he buried his face in her hair. She smelled like wildflowers and sunshine. A scent he couldn't seem to forget. He brushed his lips against her neck and smiled when he felt her tremble. "We'll figure it out."

"I'm here for the week."

He kissed her hard and quick. One week. Enough time and not nearly enough time to work toward making that temporary courtship more permanent.

Chapter Fifteen

A year later

Are you at home?

Bree texted Darren and waited. He knew she was flying in for the Fourth of July. It was her vacation, and she'd planned to come home.

Home.

Ever since she'd left for Seattle, Bree had considered Maple Springs home. It's where Darren was, and he'd become her safe place—the place where she felt the most like herself. He'd helped her become the person she longed to be. Confident and maybe even a little fearless.

Darren's presence in court had given her courage. She hadn't looked at him for fear he'd see right through her brave facade. Despite her attempt to protect both families from a trial, the Johnsons had severed their relationship with her parents that day, right before Philip's preliminary exam had started. They blamed her for everything. In the past, such an incident would have made her crumble, but she stood firm and faced them all. And justice was served.

Darren was what she wanted, and now—
She grinned and texted again.

Where are you?

Her phone whistled with an incoming message. Finally.

Give a guy a chance to respond. I'm home. Where are you?

On my way.

Bree pocketed her phone and pulled out of her parents' driveway in her mom's car. She could hardly wait to share her news. Big news, too. She hadn't seen Darren since he visited her in March. He'd come out to see her at Christmastime, too, since the symphony schedule over the holidays was crammed with concerts and she couldn't get away.

She'd had the best Christmas ever. Spent with Darren. They'd picked out a tree together and decorated it with strung cranberries and popcorn. During the in-betweens, they'd video-chatted and burned up each other's cell phone batteries. She hadn't been home since last summer. And it felt like coming home to the place she belonged. For good.

Once out of town, Bree pressed the gas pedal, eager to tell Darren so many things.

Darren looked at his two beagles sharing a big dog bed. They'd watched him buzz around his house, making sure everything was picked up and clean.

Mickey thumped his tail.

"You'll be happy to know that Bree is coming over." He'd expected her to call from the airport so he could pick her up. Evidently her parents had done that. And that was okay, he supposed.

He looked forward to telling her his news. It was big news, especially for him. He heard a knock on his door and his dogs ran toward it, barking. Pulse pounding, he followed.

Bree stood on the porch. She'd cut her rich brown hair; it hung loose and tempting at her shoulders. She'd let her bangs grow out, too, and with them pushed to the side, she looked prettier than ever. Especially wearing a sundress that hugged her slender form.

Mickey and Clara yipped with excitement.

He stared. "Wow, you look great."

"You, too." She smiled, flashing those dimples he loved. "Can I come in?"

"Of course." He laughed and backed up. "Sorry."

His dogs whined and begged for attention at her sandal-clad feet. They'd missed her, too.

Bree gave them each pats.

Darren shooed them away and pulled Bree into a hug. "I missed you."

"You have no idea how much I missed you." Bree clung to him. "And I have something to tell you."

"I have news for you, too." He kissed her, quick and hard.

Bree laughed when they broke apart. The dogs circled them both, tails wagging and yipping for attention. Their turn. She knelt down and gave each dog a hug. "Is this what you want?"

Darren ordered the dogs to their bed. They scampered to obey his master tone. He got first dibs on Bree's attention. "Come in and tell me."

She followed him to the kitchen. "Maybe you should go first."

"Want something to drink?" Darren opened the fridge and pulled out a can of pop.

Bree leaned against the counter, glowing with excitement. She waved away the can. "Later. Tell me your news."

Darren took a deep breath. He'd waited till now to tell her. "I've been interviewing with the Washington Department of Fish and Wildlife. I have a job out there."

Bree openly stared at him, and then her eyes filled with tears. "When did you interview?"

"Christmastime. I met with their captain when I was out there. I've video-conferenced a few times since."

She blinked. "But you said you'd never move."

"Things change." He smiled. *He'd* changed.

Bree still looked like she couldn't believe what he'd done. He didn't know if that was good or bad. "But what about your supervisor position here? The one you'd wanted for so long."

"I talked to my boss. I may be able to return. They can't guarantee my same position or location, but I have good internal references. I figured we'd know after a year or so where we want to be. When you finish your residency."

"Oh, Darren." Bree launched herself into him and hung on. "I don't know what to say. You'd move for me?"

He hugged her close. He'd learned that he'd move around the world and back if it meant they could be together. Forever. As much as he loved Northern Michigan, he loved her more. She'd become his home. His real home, and that's what mattered most. "Yes, Bree, I'd do that, because I love you."

"Oh, I love you, too." She pulled back and laughed. Tears streamed down her cheeks. "But you don't have to—"

Sure he did. It was time to take that next step in their relationship. "I can't do this distance anymore. Nothing matters if I can't share it with you."

She put a finger against his lips. "I'm moving here."

He grabbed her hand. "But you haven't finished the residency." He couldn't let her give that up.

She only smiled broader, and her eyes shone with excitement. "I have finished. I went as far as I wanted to go. I learned a lot. More than I ever expected. I worked hard, but the longer I stayed, the more I knew I wanted to leave. I wanted to come home."

"What about your dream to hear the music you've created played?"

"Maybe the whole reason God gave me this opportunity was to prove that my desire for fame was misplaced and not the best use of my gifts. Hearing my piece—you know, the one I played in the sugar shack—hearing it played by the strings section in Seattle wasn't what I thought it would be. Nice, sure, but empty. There was no deep, lasting impact on anyone but me. I realized that instead of trying to prove my music worthy, I need to show others why theirs is worthy. Does that make any sense?"

Maybe. He rubbed the back of his neck. "So, you quit?"

She laughed. "Not right away, but after I got a call from Jan Nelson, I sure did."

"Who's she?"

"A Bay Willows board member who is behind the Bay Willows School of Music. It's not a music camp catering to the residents' kids like I'd originally thought. Jan has some great connections, and the board decided to give her free rein. The program will be geared toward college students who want intensive training in professional development with sessions ranging from a couple of weeks to three months of study. Right up my alley. You're looking at the first faculty artist hired."

Before Darren could join in her excitement, he had to know that he wasn't the reason she'd abandoned her dreams and left Seattle. He didn't want that forever between them. "What if I had moved out there before you got this call? Would you still have taken it?"

Bree bit her lip. "I would have wanted to, but knowing you'd given up everything you loved... I don't know. I would have talked to you first, you know, and found out what you wanted to do."

Good enough. Darren opened his arms wide. "Well, then, congratulations."

She jumped into his embrace. "I'm so excited. I mean, this is a ground-floor opportunity. It's something I can grow with and help mold. I'll travel some, work with planning and admissions, but the best part is that I get to live here with something really special to do."

"Instead of just vacationing."

She pulled back and looked him straight in the eyes. She glowed from the inside out. "You're my vacation, Darren. But I need to make it permanent, if you're willing to make it so."

He knew where this was going and grinned. "Yeah? What did you have in mind?"

"I should probably wait and let you get used to having me around all the time, but...well, sometimes a woman has to brave up and ask..."

He threaded his fingers through her hair. "Ask what?"

Bree tipped her head back. "Will you marry me?"

"Funny you should ask that. Wait here." He let go of her and headed down the hall, into his bedroom, for yet another surprise.

Bree paced the kitchen floor, waiting. What was taking him so long? They'd shared so much at Christmas, and yet Darren hadn't let on that he'd been working on a way for them to be together. He'd never once asked her to give up the residency, even when she'd complained about how hard it had been.

She heard his footsteps and whipped around. She knew what he'd gone to get, but seeing that small black velvet box in his hands caused her to tear up all over again.

"I'm not giving you this if you're going to cry," his deep voice teased. Gently, ever so gently.

"I'm just happy. Darren, I never dreamed I'd be this happy. I nearly settled—"

He hushed her with his fingers against her lips, like she'd done to him earlier. "We've both made mistakes, but God had better things in mind for us. He knew we'd be *us*."

Bree sniffed. "Yes, He knew. And I love *us*."

"Me, too." Darren opened the box to reveal a beautiful solitaire diamond engagement ring. "And so, to answer your question, yes, Bree. I will marry you."

She gasped at the ring's unique setting. Two white gold swirls cradled the diamond amid folds of more white gold. "Where did you find this?"

"A new jeweler in Maple Springs designs them. I took one look at it and thought of you."

"It's gorgeous." She held out her left hand for him to slip the ring on her third finger. It fit perfectly. "How'd you know my size?"

"Your mom told me."

Bree gave him a sharp look. "She knew about this before me?"

"Hey, you're the one who proposed. I was getting ready to, clearing it with your folks and all."

"Yeah, and you've gotten pretty chummy with them from what I hear. Mom says you're over there a lot."

He shrugged. "Just making the rounds while checking on Stella."

No doubt fixing things too. Her mom had said that

Darren had helped her father with a host of little projects. "Well, thank you."

"You're welcome."

Bree stared at the ring, a pledge of their love and commitment. He'd been planning this all along. Taking his time and getting it right. Getting to know her parents, too.

She recalled Darren's poetic descriptions of the area when they'd first met. This ring reminded her of that, only warm summer moonlight instead of winter blue. He had a way of not only seeing the beauty surrounding him but also protecting it. He was music in the making, filling her with emotion that translated well into notes and chords. Inspiring her. He'd always inspired her.

God had brought them together under the guise of a wild edibles class. Little had Bree known that she was in for the experience of a lifetime. Life with Darren promised love and acceptance and her innermost dreams come true.

Epilogue

The last Saturday of the summer and it was a hot one. Standing along the shoreline of Lake Michigan's Maple Bay, Darren waited for Bree, his bride.

It was a small wedding ceremony with only their closest friends and family. Neil stood next to him, cane in hand, as Darren's best man. Bree's sister had accepted the role of matron of honor and she stood on the other side of him. Waiting, too.

Despite the stifling temperatures, a cool breeze blew in from the lake. He felt his phone vibrate with an incoming text from the depths of his pocket. He'd turned the volume off for the ceremony. Who texted him at this moment, of all moments?

It dawned on him who it might be and he grabbed the phone for a quick peek.

"What are you doing?" Neil hissed.

"It'll only take a second to check." Yup, the text came from Bree, making him smile.

For a split second, Darren's stomach flipped. What if— No. Not a chance. He read her message.

Are you ready?

Her question was followed by several hearts.

Darren chuckled. No worries about his bride showing up today. He texted her back.

Hurry up.

The music started. A gentle sound of a string quartet played something soft and sweet. He'd get to know this kind of music pretty well in the coming years. He looked forward to attending the concerts Bree would take part in and help plan.

Bree loved her new job. Loved the process of interviewing musicians for the following year when the school officially opened for their first sessions. Already they had a good roster of college and post-college students registered to attend. Darren had no doubt that this was where she was meant to be. Here in Northern Michigan, impacting the lives of others. Making a difference in his.

Finally he spotted her walking toward him on the arm of her father, and his breath caught.

She was beautiful in a simple white gown with a top of delicate lace. Pretty, like her. She didn't wear a veil. Her hair had been swirled up into a loose knot. Within the mink-colored mass, she'd tucked tiny white baby's breath that grew wild around here. She carried a bouquet of sunflowers bundled with more of the airy white wildflower.

He cleared his throat, trying to loosen the emotion that tightened it. He felt Neil's hand grip his shoulder. Darren needed to get it together. He'd have to talk if they were to exchange their vows.

But right now, all he could do was watch Bree walk toward him, her golden eyes shiny and wet. If she starting crying, he'd be hard-pressed not to join her.

So Darren scanned the guests present to get a handle

on his composure. Stella dabbed at her eyes with a tissue, as did his mom and even Bree's mom. This joy was certainly contagious.

He'd waited a long time for this moment. God had given him the right woman not only to share his life but also to open his eyes. None of them were good enough but for the grace of God. They were all God's people, whether they knew it or not.

Darren needed to serve with that in mind. Always. *To everything there is a season, and a time to every purpose under heaven.*

* * * * *

Pick up the other stories in
Jenna Mindel's MAPLE SPRINGS *series:*
Where love runs sweet

FALLING FOR THE MOM-TO-BE
A SOLDIER'S VALENTINE

And enjoy these other sweet romances
from Jenna Mindel:

MENDING FENCES
SEASON OF DREAMS
COURTING HOPE
SEASON OF REDEMPTION
THE DEPUTY'S NEW FAMILY

Available now from Love Inspired!

Find more great reads at www.LoveInspired.com.

Dear Reader,

Thank you for picking up a copy of my latest book in the Maple Springs series and the continuing tale of loss and love within the Zelinsky family. I hope you've enjoyed Darren and Bree's journey to real love.

This might have been the most difficult book I've ever written. I had quite the time getting a handle on what these two people not only wanted but also needed. In the end, it all boiled down to how they viewed themselves— incorrectly and certainly not as God saw them.

None of us are good enough outside God's grace. Only through Him and His gift of salvation are we perfected and made whole. No matter what comes our way, what hurts we've experienced in or out of our control, God can heal them if we keep our hearts tuned toward Him.

May your innermost dreams come true, and happy reading.

God bless,
Jenna Mindel

REQUEST YOUR FREE BOOKS!

2 FREE INSPIRATIONAL NOVELS
PLUS 2
FREE
MYSTERY GIFTS

Love Inspired®

YES! Please send me 2 FREE Love Inspired® novels and my 2 FREE mystery gifts (gifts are worth about $10). After receiving them, if I don't wish to receive any more books, I can return the shipping statement marked "cancel." If I don't cancel, I will receive 6 brand-new novels every month and be billed just $4.99 per book in the U.S. or $5.49 per book in Canada. That's a saving of at least 17% off the cover price. It's quite a bargain! Shipping and handling is just 50¢ per book in the U.S. and 75¢ per book in Canada.* I understand that accepting the 2 free books and gifts places me under no obligation to buy anything. I can always return a shipment and cancel at any time. Even if I never buy another book, the two free books and gifts are mine to keep forever.

105/305 IDN GH5P

Name	(PLEASE PRINT)
Address	Apt. #
City	State/Prov.	Zip/Postal Code

Signature (if under 18, a parent or guardian must sign)

Mail to the **Reader Service:**
IN U.S.A.: P.O. Box 1867, Buffalo, NY 14240-1867
IN CANADA: P.O. Box 609, Fort Erie, Ontario L2A 5X3

**Are you a subscriber to Love Inspired® books
and want to receive the larger-print edition?
Call 1-800-873-8635 or visit www.ReaderService.com.**

* Terms and prices subject to change without notice. Prices do not include applicable taxes. Sales tax applicable in N.Y. Canadian residents will be charged applicable taxes. Offer not valid in Quebec. This offer is limited to one order per household. Not valid for current subscribers to Love Inspired books. All orders subject to credit approval. Credit or debit balances in a customer's account(s) may be offset by any other outstanding balance owed by or to the customer. Please allow 4 to 6 weeks for delivery. Offer available while quantities last.

Your Privacy—The Reader Service is committed to protecting your privacy. Our Privacy Policy is available online at www.ReaderService.com or upon request from the Reader Service.

We make a portion of our mailing list available to reputable third parties that offer products we believe may interest you. If you prefer that we not exchange your name with third parties, or if you wish to clarify or modify your communication preferences, please visit us at www.ReaderService.com/consumerschoice or write to us at Reader Service Preference Service, P.O. Box 9062, Buffalo, NY 14240-9062. Include your complete name and address.

LI15

SPECIAL EXCERPT FROM

Love Inspired®

What happens when a Texas Ranger determined to stay single meets a pregnant widow who unwittingly works her way into his heart?

Read on for a sneak preview of the second book in the **LONE STAR COWBOY LEAGUE: BOYS RANCH** *miniseries, THE RANGER'S TEXAS PROPOSAL* by *Jessica Keller.*

"What can I do for you, Officer?" Josie Markham's tone said she didn't really want to do anything for him. Ever.

He raised his eyebrows.

"White hat. Boots. White starched shirt. And that belt's the type they only issue to Texas Rangers." She gestured toward his holster. "I hope you weren't trying to be undercover."

"Good eye." He extended his hand. She narrowed her gaze but shook it. "Heath Grayson. I'm a friend of Flint's."

In the space of a heartbeat, her hesitant expression vanished and was replaced by wide-eyed concern. "Did something else happen at the boys ranch?" She shifted from around the wheelbarrow. "What are we waiting for? If something's wrong, let's go."

Once she moved away from the wheelbarrow, he saw her stomach. Pregnant. Very pregnant. Flint had mentioned Josie was widowed, but he'd left out the little detail that she was with child. So a recent widow.

LIEXP1016

Had she been in the barn alone…doing chores?

"Let me help you with your chores," Heath said.

Josie's jaw dropped. "What about the boys ranch?"

"The ranch is fine."

"Why didn't you say so? You about gave me a heart attack." She laid her hand on her chest and took a few deep breaths. Then her eyes skirted back up to capture his. "If the ranch is fine, why exactly are you here then?"

She fanned her face and dragged in huge amounts of oxygen through her mouth as if she was having a hard time getting it into her lungs.

Now he'd done it. Gone and gotten a pregnant woman all worked up. Did he need to find her a chair? A drink of water? Rush her to the hospital? What a terrible feeling, being out of control. It was disconcerting.

"Are you all right, ma'am? What do you need?"

"I'm fine. Just fine." She laughed. "You should see your face, though." She pointed up at him and covered her mouth, hiding her wide grin. Her warm brown eyes shone with mischief. "Now you look like you're the one having a heart attack. Relax there, Officer. It was only a figure of speech." Her laugh was a high sound, full of joy. Josie laughed with her whole self, without holding anything back.

Heath wanted to hear it again.

Don't miss
THE RANGER'S TEXAS PROPOSAL
by Jessica Keller, available November 2016 wherever
Love Inspired® books and ebooks are sold.

www.LoveInspired.com

LIEXP1016

SPECIAL EXCERPT FROM

Love Inspired HISTORICAL

*Nora Underhill needs a husband to fend off her
overbearing family, and Simon Wallin wants the
farmland he'd earn by marrying her. Their marriage of
convenience seems like the perfect bargain...as long as
love isn't part of the deal.*

*Read on for a sneak preview of
CONVENIENT CHRISTMAS WEDDING,
by Regina Scott, available November 2016
from Love Inspired Historical!*

"There's the land office," Simon said, nodding to a
whitewashed building ahead. He strode to it, shifted
Nora's case under one arm and held the door open for her,
then followed her inside with his brothers in his wake.

The long, narrow office was bisected by a counter.
Chairs against the white-paneled walls told of lengthy
waits, but today the only person in the room was a slender
man behind the counter. He was shrugging into a coat as
if getting ready to close up for the day.

Handing Nora's case to his brother John, Simon
hurried forward. "I need to file a claim."

The fellow paused, eyed him and then glanced at Nora,
who came to stand beside Simon. The clerk smoothed
down his lank brown hair and stepped up to the counter.
"Do you have the necessary application and fee?"

Simon drew out the ten-dollar fee, then pulled the
papers from his coat and laid them on the counter. The
clerk took his time reading them, glancing now and then

at Nora, who bowed her head as if looking at the shoes peeping out from under her scalloped hem.

"And this is your wife?" he asked at last.

Simon nodded. "I brought witnesses to the fact, as required."

John and Levi stepped closer. The clerk's gaze returned to Nora. "Are you Mrs. Wallin?"

She glanced at Simon as if wondering the same thing, and for a moment he thought they were all doomed. Had she decided he wasn't the man she'd thought him? Had he married for nothing?

Nora turned and held out her hand to the clerk. "Yes, I'm Mrs. Simon Wallin. No need to wish me happy, for I find I have happiness to spare."

The clerk's smile appeared, brightening his lean face. "Mr. Wallin is one fortunate fellow." He turned to pull a heavy leather-bound book from his desk, thumped it down on the counter and opened it to a page to begin recording the claim.

Simon knew he ought to feel blessed indeed as he accepted the receipt from the clerk. He had just earned his family the farmland they so badly needed. The acreage would serve the Wallins for years to come and support the town that had been his father's dream. Yet something nagged at him, warned him that he had miscalculated.

He never miscalculated.

Don't miss
CONVENIENT CHRISTMAS WEDDING
by Regina Scott, available November 2016 wherever
Love Inspired® Historical books and ebooks are sold.

www.LoveInspired.com

LIHEXP1016